Born in 1991, Cecilie Lind studied at Forfatterskolen (The Danish Academy of Creative Writing), and debuted in 2010 with the poetry collection *Ulven åd min eyeliner* (*The Wolf Ate My Eyeliner*). Lind's breakthrough in Denmark came with the publication of the highly acclaimed book-length poem *Mit barn* (*My Child*) which was shortlisted for the 2020 Danish Critics Prize and the Politiken's Literary Award. She was awarded The Native Language Prize in 2020, and *Girlbeast* won the Danish Critics Prize in 2023. Lind's most recent novel, *Bristefærdig* (*Ripe*), was published to critical acclaim in 2025.

Hazel Evans (b. 1994) is an artist, writer and literary translator based near Aarhus, Denmark. She was the 2022/23 emerging translator for Danish to English at the National Centre for Writing, and her debut translation, *Into a Star* by Puk Qvortrup, was published by Hamish Hamilton. In 2024, she received The Inger and Jens Bruun Translation Prize for her translation of Rasmus Daugbjerg's *Troll*, forthcoming from Penguin Press.

Girlbeast

Cecilie Lind

Translated from the Danish
by Hazel Evans

Girlbeast

2038

On Christmas Eve I slip into a tight, yellow silk dress. I consider myself in the full-length mirror in the hall. My body still looks young, I'm thin, my breasts are perky. I'm freezing.

The radiator is white and cold like the moon.

They're lemons in that dress, Monika says, and gives one of them a squeeze.

Everything oozes idyll, the roast roasts in the oven. The red cabbage wafts. The tree stands naked, awaiting its hearts. I've insisted on risalamande, Monika is chopping the almonds.

I'm pressing cloves into a big, beautiful orange.

Tender finger pulp.

The cat is playing with a ball of wool at my feet.

We invited a girl in, she looked forlorn out in the snow, we recognised her from the backyard, she plays there a lot. She was wearing a thin coat, no hat. She was playing out in the snow by herself.

She cried, her mum and dad were fighting over the gravy, she said. We could hear screams from the window. We lured her in to us with a present, thought: She needs protecting. Look, we could use your help, how else will the tree become wonderful?

She gets a stool so she can reach the top, stretches, on tiptoes, just about reaches, and places a silver star there. Monika takes hold of her by the waist. Lifts her down. Light as a feather. She seems confused, stood waiting with her hand out. The present is a piece of jewellery, Monika found it in her jewellery box. A real diamond. We assure her.

It was mine.

She's thirteen and the neighbours' daughter. Poor thing, Monika says. She's not having an easy time of it.

I light the candles on the tree. My hands are shaking and I have to drag the match several times before it catches, the little flame could become the big flame, but I'm careful, as always, and all the candles are lit. The tree is perfect, and the girl gets a kiss on the cheek from Monika. A smudge of dark red lipstick. I wipe it off with a napkin I wet with spit.

It's a child's tree, my sweetheart, Monika says to her.

My name is Lisa, she says. And she turns to me, gives me a hug, says thanks, you're nice, her eyes shine brighter than the diamond than the candles.

Now she'll go into her own living room, dance around her own tree, with her mum's and dad's hands in hers. I give her my number, tell her to text me, or call, if she ever needs to talk. With a grown-up.

She gets a glittery angel in her coat pocket, Monika slips it in, a finger over her lips, shh.

The snow falls. Monika dresses up as Father Christmas, pulls me onto her lap, says, there. I lick my peppermint candy cane.

2020

I'm thirteen.

And I'm like a tree shaken through by the wind.

The birds are chirping in the garden.

I was born in a red house with long, green curtains with long, green fringes. I was born in the bath. A quick, merciful birth. I slid right out.

Like she was shelling a boiled almond, my mum.

What a birth, what a breeze, said the midwife, handing Dad the scissors with which he struggled to cut the rubbery cord.

The midwife said she'd never seen such a beautiful baby. Such bright eyes.

My mum was 39 and my dad 52 when they had me. I was the child they'd dreamt of since they met. I was a dream. What they longed to be. A family. I was their miracle.

My parents had dreamt me so much up and into their hands, into their lives, that when I finally arrived, I could only disappoint.

The dream child was enough child for them. The child I was was too pale. Too quiet by day. Inconsolable by night. Demanding. Grumpy.

I didn't shine. I wasn't a sun. The milk I regurgitated wasn't warm delight between my mum's breasts. Something to be brushed off with a wet wipe and a loving smile.

She called me, with reluctance, princess, but she never managed to convince herself of the truth of the word. Princess. The sound from their lips, in their call, hung behind me like stench. Princess settled like a crick in my neck, held my head high, proud, sick.

I grew towards the sky.

Fringe, eyes below, my fringe is a blind being lowered as slowly as death is beckoning to me.

I take a swig of milk, and regret it. The milk is sour, I spit a mouthful back into the glass.

Dad comes in, places a hand on my shoulder, hey sweetheart, he says, taking the glass and gulping it down. Seemingly immune to its taste.

I stretch my arms over my head. My breasts cast a shadow on the wall. Dad's eyes linger on the shadow a couple of seconds before finding my face, he smiles and goes into the kitchen, to Mum, who's stood watching over a meat sauce and possibly crying a bit into the pan, and they speak to each other, sharp and hushed.

We're out of cream. Mum says.

I go to the shop for half a litre. It's hot. The sweat between my breasts is bothering me. I cast about to see if there are any cyclists, slip a hand between my breasts, rub up and down a bit to get rid of the worst of the moisture. My hand slides around my left breast, takes tentatively hold, it's heavy and perky. It feels like someone else's.

This is the summer they've really grown out, and they're mine.

I'm a plant. I shoot.

I feel powerful, I feel violated.

A car drives by, it slows down, it beeps.

I stick out my tongue, probably too late. I don't think he saw. All he saw was my butt, my back, my hair, my dress.

I know this summer belongs to me. It will obey me.

And I know Mum hates me for my strong, young body and my long, light hair made even lighter by the sun.

It's so light it's nearly white.

They're sold out of cream. The shop is small and warm. Flies buzz about the fruit. The shopkeeper is counting coins, her name is Gitte. She used to be my handball coach, now she eyes my hesitation by the fridge, my superior beauty, bitterly.

I think she thinks I'm going to steal.

I return home empty-handed. Mum gives me hell, I roll my eyes.

She tells me to change into another dress. I refuse.

Summer rain heavy and mine. Like my breasts, like my future.

I go out into the weather in my white dress and let all the raindrops soak me through.

Try to be as refined as possible.

Be toxic.

If you happened to brush up against me my skin would bloom red boils.

Houses can swallow girls.

To break free, sometimes you have to smash a thing to bits. Dad's bottle of wine.

Mum sweeps the kitchen floor as quietly as she can. Then mops with soggy kitchen roll.

I hide in my room. Admonished.

I'd been cheeky, stuck my tongue out, at Mum, after being corrected, put the milk in the fridge, don't drink from the carton, my lipstick on the rim the evidence.

I held my tongue.

Refused to admit to my crime. My fingertips quivered in rage. The rest of my body was statue.

Got hold of the bottle, hit it against the kitchen counter.

She gave me a slap, it sang. Suited me.

A rising sun, a blood moon.

Tears ran from my eyes, glittered down my cheeks. They showed like snail trails in my powderskin.

The pink wallpaper. It owns me. I lie on my stomach in bed. Watch the shadow of the tree as it dances.

The birds chirp. The garden is fallen. The grass is dry and hot. The trees bear no fruit, they're in bloom now, it's summer.

I'm looking forward to the plums. The greeny-yellow ones.

I have a book in front of me. *White Fur*, lying open at chapter seven, I can't concentrate enough to read.

There's a picture of the author on the flap. She's so incredibly beautiful, her so light hair pulled tight at her nape, her gaze is strong and good, and I want to know who she is, she looks like a movie star, her exposed shoulders are perfect, but she's dead.

I wish she was my mum, I say to Mum, when Mum tells me to mow the lawn.

Mum hates that I read. So I read and read.

Mum says it's unhealthy to turn your back on reality.

My beautiful back.

Dad has a hand on it while we're sat on the sofa watching *The Birds.*

Nose never not buried in a book. It makes you strange. She says.

It's not healthy.

I borrowed the book from the library, on the priest's recommendation.

The pages are worn and yellow.

Carmen is seventeen when she falls for a forty-four-year-old philosopher. Their love is impossible and beautiful.

They have sex every ten pages.

The grass shines like elixir, my eczema blooms.

I love the little white flower that waits to become an apple. It's so insanely patient, that flower!

Bird shit on the windscreen. My dad says the clouds are threatening. I look up at them and picture them as puffed sleeves.

I was the result of fertility treatment. The fruit.

A gruelling and undignified process.

Said my mum to her mum.

I found the papers, they were hidden away in a shoebox, it was on top of the wardrobe.

That's how you stay safe.

Shut up.

In the box there was also a photo from my christening.

The ceremony took place at the cathedral, the young, beautiful priest who poured water over my head as I screamed blue murder, in my grandma's arms, she was a witness, fucked me so well and earnestly fourteen years later that I lost my heart to him.

He came to the party at my parents' house afterwards, the guest of honour. He proposed a toast to my future, to the life that lay ahead of me and was mine to be lived.

She'll be good, smart and loving, I can tell, he said, and beautiful, trailing his finger over my little forehead.

My mum was touched he'd taken the time to join us at the table. With that busy schedule of yours, she said to him, a hand on his shoulder. He smiled his warm smile at her and said: But of course.

My mum noted how meticulously the priest folded his name card and tucked it into his pocket, she'd been up half the night painting them. He's a good man, she thought, her cheeks warm.

Shrimp cocktail was the starter, roast lamb the main, pavlova and redcurrants the dessert.

I'm pure. I tell my mum, I'm pure.

She accuses me, calls me a naughty girl.

Mum has a hard time believing me. A girl as pretty as you, she says, sighs, can't expect to walk the streets in peace. You must have been a little, willing pig. You must have succumbed to the temptation of a big, furry hand when it brushed your back, and you turned around and smiled, the man's red mouth didn't alarm you but pulled you into it, trapped you in a kiss that turned to fire between your legs, the hand found its way down into your underwear, past your tight trousers, the hand could just about fit, and you were all wet, and the man says, moans, Sara, you're so wet, you're so horny, but you don't respond, you let him carry on, let his fingers find their way into you, and you welcome them, like a big mouth is your cunt, like a big hungry fish if you dipped your finger into the fish tank at the florist's, you close in on those fingers, you're tight and unsullied, and he can hardly contain himself in his excitement, his desire, he wants to put more into you, into the narrow, young hole that you are.

That's what men want. Mum says.

They want to force themselves into your openings and knock you up.

Sara, are you listening to me, Mum shakes me, get it into your head.

I make no attempt to resist.

It's so hard, it's so hard, Dad is saying to Mum. I overheard them talking, they thought I was asleep, hot and small in my bed, but I woke, hot and small and wide awake, and thirsty, tiptoed down the stairs and heard my name, avoided the creaky step, Dad's voice, Mum's quiet, listening.

It's so hard to tell her off, she doesn't know any better, there's a fragility to her, like she'd shatter like nothing, like she's the skin of a boiled almond. If we were to plant shame in her, and if that shame were to take root, I wouldn't be able to live with myself. Wouldn't be able to look myself in the eye, Dad says and looks Mum in the eye, Mum looks down.

Leave her alone, Dad says. He meant it.

I mean it. Dad says.

Mum hisses,

shut up.

Dad hits.

Dad only hit Mum to be my shield. The heat of his palm against her pale cheek.

Mum cried herself to sleep, I heard through the wall.

Dad usually took my side. Dad didn't let Mum's whims affect me, if he could help it.

Mum said I had him wrapped around my little finger. That I manipulated him. That we turned on her. As allies.

The child was never meant to be her sacrifice, the child was meant to be her angel.

Her everything.

Her salvation, purpose, armour.

Her friend.

Her pet, her god.

A fur to lick, a pair of feet to throw herself at.

All I give rise to in her is bad conscience. Anger. Anger boiling over. Shame. A feeling of not enough.

Slut, Mum hissed. I had entered the living room, radiant and fierce in my short, red dress. And then came the little confession, what she'd cost at sixteen.

A dress. A piece of jewellery.

But I was hoping for his heart.

I didn't want to know. She flipped out. Threw a lemon at me, it flew past my head, hit the wall, a little thump like a neighbour wanting to know what was going on, a little, feeble fist helpless against the woodchip wallpaper before falling down onto the red rug, and the yellow against the red was beautiful. I cried, but it was a bewildered cry, I had no idea how else to respond.

She wasn't in her right mind, Dad said, forgive her, she didn't mean to hurt you. Just let her console you. Please. Sweetheart.

For Dad's sake I let her kiss me goodnight that night. A kiss on the forehead. Still mad at her.

She whispers: Sorry.

I say: It's ok, Mum.

The evil line around her mouth sets in.

She says: But you –

She says it's not her fault I'm so rude and defiant.

She takes her sorry back.

Expects one from my lips.

Sorry.

Mum left.

Dad came in, whispering,

THANK YOU.

Silent night, holy night. He sings. With my hand in his.

He's hoping for a peaceful night on the sofa.

He leaves my room when he thinks I'm sleeping, but I'm not sleeping.

I'm thinking.

I want to sneak out, run away, take refuge, but where to go? Who would understand?

Care?

Protect?

I think of the priest, of his eyes, and of his smile. Friendly, soft. And the light in his eye. I know that if I'm to be saved, he'll be the one to do the saving.

His hands clasped in his lap. The gold ring on his ring finger. Those broad shoulders.

Wish I had real problems, wish he'd notice my shoulder blades, on their way to wings. Wish he could see the horns I feel budding in my forehead. He has laid his hand there, a blessing, he has felt them. They have scared him.

Egged him on. Too.

And my breasts.

Hehe.

The priest sent me a photo of a poppy field. I'd told him I love poppies. It was elation to receive that photo. Look where I am, he wrote.

Paradise ♥

I replied.

Knowing full well it was his wife's mum's summer house.

He calls her

my spouse.

15:37 Wish you were here

15:43 To see it

15:50 The poppies

I don't reply.

I'm painting my toenails light blue.

The holidays are clinging to me like a silk dress.

I'm so sublime now that school has left me in peace and the other girls from my class are eating biscuits in camper vans away from here. The crumbs in the sheets don't bother them. Their seasoned silky backs lounge on sunbeds in gardens as fathers and mothers serve juice and drink white wine. A burnt neck, a sunkissed calf. The sunhat forgotten in the park. I'm calm. The calm fuels my desire. A green pear in my hand is all I need to be queen. A beach is a stage. I read in the sand, turning golden and warm. The sun is a blanket laid over me by God. He sees me. Looks after me. Sunshine turns me on.

I've built myself a little sandcastle to lie on. It lifts my butt slightly up. My black swimsuit crawls between my cheeks.

My party is the waves and the seagull and the mussels and the woman stretching by the water. Her poodle barks at the sea. It thinks it has an enemy.

At 18:07 I answer: I wish.

After five and after ten and after twenty minutes he hasn't replied.

I keep reading *White Fur*.

Darkness falls, the sun melts into the sea.

The most beautiful mussel in my pocket.

Then I ride home. Force myself not to look at my phone, see if he's answered, not until midnight, at midnight I can look, I abstain.

I get home late, and Mum and Dad don't notice. They're snapping at each other on the sofa as the news is read out by a man with a dead gaze, cleft chin. Electricity prices are rising. Nurses are striking.

Dad snorts, Mum glowers at him. I tiptoe into my room.

Had been waiting by the microwave for the tomato soup to heat up.

Breathe a sigh of relief.

Safety.

Leave the soup until it's cold, then water my houseplant with it.

Mum looks in before going to bed, her face has turned smooth and soft, and she looks happy when she sees the empty bowl, red dregs at the bottom. Goodnight, my girl, she says, leaves the door ajar. I have to get up to shut it.

Summer darkness is a feeble kind of darkness, it never quite takes hold, is more of a glaze, a glaze that glistens, a gloss that draws everything a bit closer to everything else, the cows, the flowers. The stars. Everything that teems wants to cling together. The stars want to be taken down. They're bored up there. They're mine.

I can reach up for them and not reach.

Everything is mine and is taken from me.

That's what it means to be a girl.

I write that in my diary.

Everything is camping! I shout out the window. Frightening a cyclist. It jolts him, nearly topples him. Then he looks up at my window and sees my little face and smiles. I smile.

I laugh and laugh, alone in my room, the laughter makes me giddy. I'm unstoppable.

Ready to burst. Overripe. A blueberry, its skin beginning to crack.

Lana Del Rey sings.

White Dress.

It's 00:06 and he hasn't replied.

I feel like writing to Rosa, but Rosa's made it clear that's no longer an option. I have to shut the fuck up. She said.

You're dust to me.

I try to sleep but can't sleep. It's like something is waiting to happen, something wild and life-changing, if only I could catch whatever is thrown at me, not try to dodge it. If only I could wear the most perfect dress to the most perfect party. If the most right man could see me, and see how I light up, then the world will reveal itself to me, and I will conquer it.

Then my phone lights up, like it's sending me an angel, and it's him, he writes,

Sleep tight.

I send the heart.

Butterflies and fire.

I want Rosa to myself. But Rosa hasn't forgiven me for telling Emilie about our kiss. Emilie wasn't that interested in my confession and soon forgot about it, spared it a shrug, she was headed home to seven newborn kittens and her heart was with them, and their mum, her beloved cat Sol, but Rosa felt betrayed, paraded, embarrassed.

So now Rosa is lost.

Rosa can't stand losing face. Rosa's shame is my shame.

She doesn't own up to her blushing, she decorates me with it, like it's my fault.

I saw her with Yrsa, they were walking hand in hand down the street. They didn't acknowledge me. My little, brittle hi hung in the air and was a ghost.

Yrsa looked satisfied and sedate. Like a gross, fat, slick cat. Like a big overripe tomato. I almost couldn't resist the urge to stick out a leg, see her trip, scrape her pointy knee bloody.

Meanwhile, the shop's clothing rails were like strange heifers, munching on the clothes they bore.

The dresses are letters to me. I am their raison d'être. I never buy them. But they're green and tender. They want what's best for me, they want to accentuate my cleavage, show off my waist. Says the woman trying to sell me one, it costs 800 kroner and I think that it's too expensive and too grown-up. That Mum would never allow it.

I won't bother.

I've stopped asking Mum for clothes, things. If I ask her in one of her better moments, she's all generosity, of course, she says, smiles, nods. Anything for you, daughter.

When I leap into her embrace, let her throw her arms around me, and my gratitude is genuine and a squeal of delight, then Mum melts, and can stand me. If I'm affectionate, helpless. Grateful.

If I make an effort I have no trouble resembling the daughter who is the dream daughter, then she has me, almost.

Then it's almost good.

Good.

Dad rolls his eyes, all that money Mum acts like we have, well, we don't.

I crush a stinging nettle in my hand. A beautiful summer's day. My sunglasses are Rosa's.

Later, at Emilie's birthday party, when Rosa and I are doing our best to act like the other doesn't exist, even though we're sitting opposite each other at the beautifully laid table, I notice Yrsa in the dress I didn't get. She's sitting at Rosa's side, affectionate and birdlike. She whispers something in Rosa's ear, and Rosa's smile is more like a grimace, and I can tell Yrsa bores her to death. She's licking her lips like she does when she wishes she was elsewhere.

Her very dark red lipstick is a thing she's trying out. The rest of us haven't yet dared with that colour, it's always Rosa who sees something, sees pictures on the internet, and knows what's beautiful, and then it is beautiful, and right, to have a dark red mouth, but when the rest of us, when I, paint our lips to look like Rosa, like Rosa's pictures, we end up looking like jokes, it doesn't work, the mouths fall to the ground, and Rosa hovers in a quiet and refined way.

We squeal over the kittens, how cute they are, they totter from girl to girl, there are six small black ones, they haven't yet opened their eyes, when I have the one with white paws in my hands I want to squeeze it, hard. Until it screams.

I kiss it on the head, little puss.

The mother meows her protest into Emilie's room, she's calling her babies to her, Emilie's mum has shut the door so we can play with the kittens in peace.

On Monday all our mouths are dark red, by Thursday Yrsa is the only one still trying. Rosa's done with her, that's obvious, but she's not yet ready to forgive me.

Sending looks that are half hateful, half begging.

I feel bad for her. Her pride is ruining everything.

I act like I'm indifferent. Moved on. Really I long for reconciliation.

Being Rosa's friend is protection, no girl can touch me when I'm Rosa's chosen one. Her love is a shiny piece of jewellery.

The boys see me better.

The girls whisper less.

Yrsa's dad is rich, that's what Rosa said. The dress doesn't suit her.

When it turns black in Mum's head, heart, her present, her little sacrifice, comes to mind, when I misbehave, if I'm disrespectful, and wearing the yellow silk she let me have, then she'll eye the silk, maybe spot a little stain, say: You don't deserve it, you don't take care, you'll get it ripped to bits, I know you will, you don't give a damn that I spent 1,000 kroner on you that I could have spent on myself.

You don't respect me.

Shame on you.

A little pinch of the arm.

The mother cat's nip of the neck when the kittens are to be put in the basket, nudged to all her nipples.

Mum got angry, I was stupid enough to tell her about Rosa's cold shoulder. I couldn't stomach Mum's indignation. Her disappointment that I couldn't even hold on to my friend.

But Mum's anger was all ablaze.

Like she was the one who'd been betrayed.

But it was really too good to be true, says Mum, to Dad, when she thinks I can't hear her, that a girl like Rosa would be able to put up with Sara.

Sara is so pale. Timid.

Beautiful Rosa. Sweet Rosa. Good Rosa. Clever Rosa.

Mum thinks Rosa is wonderful. Perfect.

I'm better off alone.

I say to Mum.

This is how I make friends with girls: I declare the girl the lady, I am slavish and dogged, I throw myself at her feet. Solicit her friendship, her favour. I subordinate myself, I suffer and rejoice. The less she cares for my worship, the more devout I become. I will do anything to win her heart, this holy heart, this girl's, anything. I'm wretched. I'm a laughing stock. I don't care. I woo. I give all of me.

And am rejected. I'm far too hungry for the alchemy of friendship. Too openly enthralled. Become a doormat. Put up with anything as long as I'm not left out. As long as Rosa will put up with me.

Fetch me a glass of water, Sara, Rosa says with a devilish look, and I fetch it, and Rosa says, I'm not thirsty after all, put it back.

This is our game of subjugation we always play.

Dad asked us to pick gooseberries from the gooseberry bush in the garden, Rosa said: Rather die.

Dad blushed.

Rosa's belly button had just been pierced, in secret, even though her dad had no objections, a sparkly stone below the hem of her crop top.

Dad doesn't have the heart to tell me off.

But for your sake – ok – Rosa and Dad and I picked and picked in silence. Dad's face was red and wet with exertion. Rosa's hands bled a bit, she'd cut herself. Stains on her white clothes. Had to borrow one of my dreseses.

It looks better on me. She said. I gave her that, it was true. Gave her it. Keep it.

It's Rosa's ankle chain I want to own. It's her yellow silk dress with the red roses on I want to go to a party in. It's her eyeshadow I want to paint my eyelids with.

Her dad I want to purr for. Be stroked by.

He's hot. Emilie said. When he picked Rosa up from Amalie's party.

Ew,

I said.

Thinking of his mouth around the cigarette. His white vest.

When he lifted me down from a tree.

I want to get so close to her I almost become her. So the

boys who fall in love with her fall in love with me too.

The movies she loves, I love. The books she loves, I love.

I want to erase her so I can become more Rosa than Rosa.

But she was the one who stole my hairband. She was the one who read my diary without permission.

She was the one who kissed me on the mouth, a kiss I didn't return, I just stood, upright, unmoving, until that kiss, it ended.

Rosa regretted it. She said: Leave me alone. She gave me a shove in the stomach and left me in the rain in the park.

I didn't run after her.

Her ponytail swung skittishly back and forth.

I can't forget the heat of the kiss. The dizziness after it. The nausea.

I had to get home and wash my mouth a thousand times with a pink flannel. My first kiss fell apart, now I'd forever be reminded of Rosa's angry lips.

We'd been queens together.

The swings were our thrones. We ordered the other girls around. Let them teem about us. Small, eager animals.

We bought necklaces made of sugar candy, ate them slowly, gnawing at our jewellery until only the string hung around our necks.

We were the it girls. The boys pulled at our hair, blushed and looked and looked at us. The girls wanted our places, wanted our hair, eyes. Most of all: our approval.

What we had in common was that we were little snacks. Everyone deified us. And hated us.

In tight dresses and lipstick. Called into the headmaster's office. Don't dress so provocatively. Belly buttons shouldn't be on display. Breasts shouldn't distract.

The boys. The men.

You?

I asked Jens, the headmaster, his forehead shiny with sweat.

He mumbled something about THE EFFECT.

Here come the dolls. Said our form teacher. Julie. We giggled our way into getting sent out. Julie's index finger pointing at the door with the poster of the royal bloodline. OUT!

Rosa's mum died when Rosa was three. Rosa can't remember her. Only that she was perfect. An angel, Rosa's dad calls Rosa's mum.

He misses her. Said Rosa. Rosa said that some nights she can hear her dad crying. He sobs into his pillow. But he always acts like nothing. In the morning. He has red eyes, and he pours his oats. He pours Rosa's cornflakes. Milk. Some sugar. He plaits Rosa's hair, and her plait is long and tight.

She's his only child.

The apple of my eye, he calls her. Sweetheart.

One and only.

Rosa has a picture of her mum on her windowsill. Next to the picture is a cactus in bloom. Three white flowers. Her mum's smile is big, white teeth. Her hair is dark and long, her eyes are brown. She's so beautiful, I said when I saw it. Rosa said: Yes.

I look like her. Rosa said.

In the picture she's standing in a forest in a red coat, it was taken before she gave birth to Rosa, right after she met Rosa's dad. The leaves are red like her coat. Her cheeks are red like the leaves like her coat.

I don't think Rosa looks like her.

I'm jealous of the dead good mum Rosa has.

And the beautiful living dad.

I'm beautiful now too, but not many people have noticed it. Yet. But I can see it in the mirror. In Rosa's scrutinous eyes. I'm more beautiful than the other girls. Even than Rosa. She's begun to admit it. Her admission makes her crueller and more obsessed with me. I look exquisite.

I'm bored.

A late summer afternoon is a terror. A torrid time stood still. Flies in the living room, buzzing, and the clock is ticking. *Wheel of Fortune* on TV or ads. Mum's reading a magazine in her bed, and Dad's gone. Out running, maybe.

NOBODY UNDERSTANDS ME
I write to the priest.
GOD LOVES YOU
he replies.
FUCK GOD
I write.
Are you ok?
the priest writes.
I send him a heart.
He sends back two.
Two hearts.
God is big
the priest writes.

Your dick is.

I write.

I regret it, but the message is sent, the insanity of boredom made me do it, there's nothing to be done.

I throw the phone away, onto the bed, the rosebud duvet screams its roses out from underneath it.

I feel like drowning myself in the sea. I want to scratch my arms bloody.

Bite a hole in my lip.

Shame drives me out of the house.

I have a loose red dress on, bare legs. I walk and walk, stay out until evening falls, Mum hasn't written. The fields are beautiful, they're being reaped now, small mice scurry to their deaths in the machines. Those small babies and their mothers. A bloodbath, a summer massacre. Nobody cries for those mice. Except me. The clouds turn pastel pink, coloured by the sun, it's art, it's blood from true hearts bleeding, bleeding blush to me.
Nature redeems me.
The waves lap at my ankles at the water's edge, where it cools, where it soothes. The beach loves me.
The shame.
The desire to see the priest's face when he sees those words. Maybe his wife is in the same room, on the same sofa. Maybe his daughter.

Your dick is.
It's moist between my legs.
Sweat beads on my forehead.

I smile.

My milk teeth lie in a pink porcelain box. There was my smile.

They're gilded. It was my confirmation gift, my parents' wish for me, as they wrote in the card: For you to bear the joy of childhood with you into adulthood. Then they handed me the box. And I didn't know what to say, but said thank you, not quite able to conceal my disappointment.

They'd made an effort.

Said Dad, they'd thought to give me something that meant something, said Mum.

More than money.

They wanted their daughter to bear her teeth around her neck.

A little child's smile.

Mum was nervous and blushing.

Fishing for my heartfelt thanks.

She looked at me like I was her executioner.
Like I was actually about to kill her.

Daughter power.

She said my name but gave up halfway;

SA–

I opened myself to her and let her stroke my arm and let her love sink in through my skin.

Cream.

Soft, white skin, little, sweet girl.

She said.

Thanks, Mum, that much I managed, Dad smiled, pulled me into a hug.

Young lady. He said.

All grown up. Said his sister.
My mum's tears rolled quietly down her cheeks, down through the thick layer of powder.

Everything about that day was awkward. The napkins folded into fans on plates, the tough lamb steak, the portioned-out ice cream. My dress with ruffles, way too many ruffles. Puffed sleeves, tutu skirt. There weren't many guests, and it was obvious they all wanted to get going. Before it gets dark, said Grandma. We sang one song. One Dad had written, the words didn't fit the melody. No one made a speech, Mum stood and proposed a toast, she was so nervous. My clever daughter. She managed to say. My sweet.

The best thing about that day was kneeling for the priest in the church. The best thing was the words he wrote in my Bible:

I am the light of the world. Whoever follows me will not walk in darkness but will have the light of life.
John 8:12

And under that, the miracle: his phone number.

After the guests left I counted the money I'd received. Not enough to tell anyone how much. Ate a box of chocolates. Not a rose from Rosa. Not even a nod at church.

Her dad greeted me with one hand on my hip, how lovely you are, Sara.

Rosa shot him a look.

My mother-of-pearl powder camouflaged my blush.

Mum had made me up. Taken my face in her hands, kissed the tip of my nose, said: Now I'm going to make you so lovely so lovely.

Trust me.

I'm stood on the beach forgetting myself. A man goes past, he's walking his dog, a black Labrador. Its tongue hangs out of its mouth, it wags. The man tries to call it to him. SALLY, he shouts in anger. The dog runs towards the sea. She ignores his call.

They don't exist.

All that exists is the thought of the priest thinking of me.

A razor clam by my foot.

Wish his dreams would find my lips. Wish my lips would wriggle free of my face and crawl over his skin, like red larvae, slime trail in their wake, my saliva, small, glistening paths. My lips crawl into the priest's mouth, they lay eggs under his tongue, the little eggs look like little pearls, the priest's tongue broods on the pearls, broods and broods until they hatch out, and out is kiss, for my forehead, my hand.

This white hand, I hold it up to the red sun, it's setting now, the sea is sinking it. It's a big, glistening sweet, the sea is a big, glistening throat. My hand is like a porcelain doll's: too white, too weak, too delicate.
That time I broke two fingers.

They're fine again, now, no one can tell.
Unless they know.

Mum knows.

The priest's cupped palm, oh, how it awaits my schoolgirl knee. Oh, how my knee longs to settle into it. God's powers of creation had an eye for romance. Innocent little girls, fully grown men. A perfect design, knee in hand, bird in nest.

Hard to imagine a sleepier beauty in the eyes of a bird.
Fed up with worms.
A little baby fallen from the nest. Save it. But it doesn't want anything to do with me. Its mum has given up. Now its baby stinks of human. It can't be taken back. Left behind for the mouth of a hungry cat.

I come to myself, realise time has run away from me.

Fuck.

This cut is begging for a plaster.

I tripped over a stone on the way home, I was walking as fast as I could, didn't want to cause alarm, the late evening had hidden a stone in its darkness. The blood ran from my knee like Mum's tears.

Mum is waiting at home, the light is on. She's twitching, her left eye a little tic, where in the world –

I roll my eyes.

Mum says:

Once you shat yourself on a pink play mat, once you drank from my breast.

Your eyes are mine.

Don't you forget it.

Don't you ever forget it.

It's your daughterly duty. If your body forgets it, it forgets me.

Sara, I love you. She spreads her arms wide to receive me.
I stay where I'm stood. Still.

I'm nauseous, I throw up, red vomit, because I ate strawberries and milk this morning.

Dad got home. A while ago. He's asleep.

We can hear his snores through the wall. Mum says:
Well well.
Are you sick?
What happened to your knee?

The next morning the carpet looks like a crime scene. Who killed a little animal in dreams? Where is the bird's corpse? A lark? A starling?
Nightingale!

I've got the hiccups and hiccup as I rub at the stain, the colour spreads, the stain grows larger, pinker.

Dad wakes up,
Mum is mad.
No one smiles.
All three of us stand with cups of coffee in hand.

The taste of coffee hangs on my lips like lipstick. I made it my mission, in this summer, in this heat, to learn to like the taste of coffee.

I want to be woman.

No, alien.

Preferably beautiful. Just beautiful.

That's all I want.

Utterly forsaken. Utterly otherworldly.

It's easier to be bold when you're beautiful. It's so easy to get away with absolutely anything, if you're beautiful.

Smile.

Said Rosa to me. She was reclining on the white daybed in the living room. A fly was buzzing. A curtain was fluttering, it's blue, the light penetrates it with such ease.

Light steps through the living room, the cat is grey. But its paws white. It purred. Its whiskers were full of cobwebs. A little mouse corpse lay rotting under the chest of drawers in the hall, several days passed before we localised the smell.

Ew. Mum screamed.

I stroked her arm, tiny, featherlike hairs. Rosa let me stroke.

The caress reconciled us. We're kittens. We are the gentle moon girls with the pink bows. Tied tight. Plaited tight. Rosa's plait is a rope, I had it in my hand. Your thick hair, Rosa, your thick lips, Rosa. Your thin arms. Your slender wrist, Rosa. You could be broken, so easily.
You could be a porcelain doll in my bedroom, on my ornament shelf, Rosa.
You could fall.

Rosa?

We are one, Sara, we are the same.

We are traps.

We are children.

Fourteen-year-old roses.

Nails are thorns.

Thorns are weapons.

Weapons are jewellery.

Jewellery is money.

Money is men's.

Men are ours.

Rosa was chewing a piece of gum, synthetic and sweet is the smell, it spreads to fill the living room, from her mouth. I held my hand out to Rosa, palm cupped right under her lips, spit, I said, and Rosa spat, the clump of gum was so big and sticky, I took it in my mouth, chewed and stared up at the ceiling, all the brown knots in the wood.

I swallow. I tell Rosa we should cut off the plait. To my surprise, she agrees. She fetches the kitchen scissors. I cut. Stand with the plait in my hand and feel like I've committed a crime.

Pretty. She says. Brings her hand to her head. The mirror shines of Rosa. She looks happy.

My luminous hair goes all the way to my butt.

Fire.

The priest is suffering in his bed.

A girl is egging him on.

Luring.

His dick is hard and big and wicked.

His dick's longing is a trial.

Satan breathes onto his window, he draws a heart with his right index finger in the condensation. Blurs it out with his hand.

Punches his clenched fist into his pillow.

To forgive sin you must know sin.

Who whispered that in his ears?

Me of course.

I can do that.

The laughter is the sea's. The waves crash and the beach bites off yet another sunset. I wonder if the punishment could be a kiss on the tip of a dick crying salt.

I wonder if God sees everything.

God sees everything.

The message lit up his night like a star.

A guiding star? Can he think of it as that?

I've sent an invitation.

His heart itches.

He wrings his hands and tries to conjure me in his mind's eye.

My narrow waist between them. The big, heavy breasts. Soft, open face.

A dream.

And then a reality:

He sees me on the beach.

I see him first. Butterflies in my stomach. Hands clenched. Pretend not to have seen, not to have noticed him.

I'm wearing the red dress.

Shy, I look down. An age since we last saw each other. My confirmation, in spring.

Right.

Now it's August.

Now the moon is large and round. I'm taller and straighter and wonderfuller.

Than then.

Those big, blue eyes. The priest's, mine.

They meet.

We have the same eyes, says the priest, that's funny. He says there's something on my cheek, a little animal, may I? He removes it, a gentle finger brushes a little insect off, I stand dead still. A jellyfish has washed up, it lies at our feet, looks like the heart of a ghost.

Skin shining. We're pale like moonlight.

I wait for the priest to say,

So –

But his hand is still on my cheek. He doesn't take it back.
Its heat makes me giddy.

It's true that the moon can bear witness.
And what does the moon see now?
Does it see?

It doesn't judge. It sanctions.

Incites.

What's happening is meant to happen. It whispers.

Like a guardian angel.

The priest says:

How strange. That you're here. Now.

A sign?

I say. And laugh.

He says:

Last night it rained. I couldn't sleep. I thought of God, first, then of you. My angel.

I remembered what you said to me about forgiveness – that it didn't apply to you – that you weren't a daughter of God, but of the devil.
To forgive me would be in vain. You said, you said: I'd pick the little baby bird up, its mum is calling from the nest, and I wouldn't, like I imagine other girls would, hold it in my hand, run a dainty finger over its little head, those dark little eyes blinking (in terror?) and cry over its fate, I wouldn't bathe it in my tears, I wouldn't squeeze it close to my heart, or feel grief, feel guilt that I in my eagerness to console and rescue have contaminated the baby with my scent, and now its mum definitely won't want anything to do with it. I would never wallow in a feeling of care and torment. I'd just, you said, if I saw that baby bird on the pavement, by the hedge, crush it to death with my foot, its leftovers clinging to my sandal. Feathers. Sticky blood.

You looked worried when you said it.
But not afraid.

But I saw, said the priest, I saw that you wanted the best for that bird. You wanted to put it out of its misery. You're not capable of letting it suffer. You wanted to bring about an end to suffering, not to the baby bird. That makes you good. Beautiful.

You're a clever and sensitive girl, that's what I wanted to tell you.

Something about you scares me.

If I brushed your skin with a feather it would leave a mark. Merely to caress your skin would be violence.

It wouldn't take much, you're easy to harm.

I held myself back, I didn't dare ask you to meet me again.

Just the two of us.

But that's what I wanted.

To see you again.

Take care of you.

That time I placed a wafer on your tongue. You swallowed. Asked for another, I laughed. Gave you ten. To go. Flesh. You ran into my arms. Sought consolation. I didn't dare hold on to you. But I wanted to.

Shh, my girl, my little girl.

The priest says.

He gently lifts one of the straps of my dress, lets it slide, halfway down my shoulder, and the other strap, he lifts that too, and it slides, halfway down my shoulder.
The moon sees my big, white breasts. They're like a mirror.
The moon sees itself.
The priest sees a miracle.
An epiphany:
Beauty. Breasts.

Between them, a heart of silver.
Breasts.
So big, young, heavy. Pale, rose.
Porcelain. Flesh.
Heavy droplets, heavy rain, heavy breathing.
Mine still.
He flays me of my pale yellow panties.
They lie on the dark sand like a white flag.
Soft feathers.
His dick rises. It sniffs.
The priest is consumed by me. I'm all appetite. Whet.
How tight you are, that's his moan.
Almost a rattle.

Pussy.
He says.
Dick.
He says.

A belly button. The sperm abandoned there, a pool. He pulled out of me. He came. He screamed.

I loved it.

The stars beam. I'm as quiet as a girl looking at a flower. My terror is also joy. I won't give him my tears. I've fallen in love with him, I fell long ago. He's the closest I'll ever come to God. My wickedness shields me from harm. I'm not easy to hurt, I'm easy to please. All I want is to lie naked on the beach, always, and stretch my hand up to the sun, and spread my fingers, and see the sun's light through them, and know that no person can ever hurt me. All the armbands and rubber rings the children float around in. They'll explode.

The sun will melt. The flames will lick.

We lie side by side, on our backs, on the sand, looking up at the sky, the stars. The priest's hand heavy on my stomach.

I can feel my blood, it's hot. I've kidnapped the priest into evil. I won.

How will he clasp his hands now, and pray his sins forgiven?

My power is violent and eternal.

I am sunwarm and eveningwonderful.

The priest holds a finger to my lips, he smiles like a child, like a conspirator. What have we done, you, what just happened? Hey.

Baby.

We wash our hands in the sea, it's so cold now. He takes my hands in his, rubs them like Mum used to rub them.

I was five, and I refused to put my mittens on. Mum said: We'll bring them with us in my pocket, I screamed NO, but let her slip the pink mittens into the pocket of her big, black coat, trod out into the snow, and we played with the snow, threw snowballs at each other. I thought Mum looked so beautiful with snowflakes in her long, dark hair, and still I refused the mittens, and my hands got cold, red and frosty, so I cried on the way home, and my mum didn't mention the mittens but took both my hands in hers and rubbed and rubbed and rubbed, is it helping? I nodded.

Don't tell a soul, Dario says, little girls have secrets, mystery, it makes them more beautiful. More important. Our secret is a secret worth keeping, because it's so pure and perverse.

You must be the angel God promised he'd send.

A strange name, for a priest, I said to him at confirmation class, before he'd suckled on my breasts on the beach, hair slung over my shoulder, pencil in hand, I was taking notes, on Jesus. He sacrificed himself for our sins, said Dario at the blackboard, at the rectory, he took the punishment upon himself. All I'd written was: He sacrificed himself for our sins. I'd drawn hearts around the sentence. I drew roses around the hearts, and ghosts around the roses. I forgot to pay attention. Dario's voice was music, not revelation.

Sara.

Dario said my name, his voice loud, harsh, strict, but when he met my gaze he smiled, playful. Where did you go? Did I lose you? What are you thinking about? I said: Nothing. I blushed. Then I said that Dario was a strange name for a priest. He nodded, and I took his smile home to bed with me.

I lay on my pillow, rubbed up against it, my orgasm like an egg being hatched.

Soft, warm, sticky.

Rosa asked: But who are we, who is our sins?
Dario said: We are man. We are children of God.

God is daddy, Rosa wrote in her notebook. We were sitting at the same table, our arms brushing. I'd lent her my red glitter gel pen. She didn't think much of Dario, he had something yellow, creamy in his beard, didn't you see? Ew. He's such a creep.

But he's kind of cute though?

He's old.

Rosa's disgust made my love more determined.

I took her hand in mine when we left, when we went by the petrol station for sweets, we walked and whistled, and our hands held each other like they were holding the world together, ugh, a big, fat, yellow caterpillar, look, it's got hair, a little white cat, aww, Rosa might say, and I'd look. Look at this red lollipop, she'd say, and I'd crush it between my teeth as she ate a chocolate button, as her cheeks were red with laughter, and as the movie played. The light of the TV. Little nighttime friendship sun.

Poison Ivy.

Fish Tank.

I slept over at hers.

I eat a litre of ice cream as I watch Rosa eating ice cream, despising myself as I lift the spoon to my mouth, as the ice cream melts in my mouth, as Rosa's ice cream is pink like her pink eyeshadow. Rosa has no shame about eating ice cream, she eats her ice cream like it were medicine, a bitter cure. An achievement. Like it's honest work. She brings the ice cream to life. Spoon by spoon. Finally the bowl is shiny, impossible to see what it used to contain. Rosa has licked it clean.

Her tongue is small, red and pointy. A flag.

She's a little calf.

She's an entire nation.

Lovely, Mum said, the first time she met her, at my place, I'd lured her home to me, promised her that in my house we'd be left in peace, my parents never kept watch, her hair in a ponytail, my mum's freshly baked bread, my mum's annoying deference.

Hold on to her, Mum said. She's a good girl. Very pretty.

And I saw Mum's longing for Rosa. For a daughter like her.

Rosa's dad said: Don't stay up all night, and we stayed up all night. The stars shone bright in the sky.

Rosa took off her nightie, told me to massage her back, I straddled her butt, grabbed her hard. She was tense. You're full of knots, Rosa. I'll loosen you up. Her muscles were strong and guarded, then she began to relax, my small, strong hands went to work, she tensed her buttcheeks, I felt it, my knees pressed gently into her waist, the oil smelled of lavender, my mum's favourite scent, Rosa said.

I thought of my grandma, her underwear drawer. Little bags of dried flowers, lavender, rose, lying between the silk, such fine panties, Grandma said, I stole a bag of tiny roses but was so ashamed of my theft I hid the bag in one of my winter boots, it's lying at the bottom of the wardrobe, putting me on edge. I'm so afraid Mum will find it, the roses crushed to powder, the whole wardrobe stinking of rose. But no one besides me seems to have noticed.

Rosa was beautiful. Her skin shone like the stars, she was pale and her spine was visible under her skin, it looked like a mighty plant, I traced its length, a finger over each vertebra. Counted them. You're so thin, Rosa, I said. I was full of admiration, respect, and Rosa said, not as thin as you, Sara.

I protested her verdict, but my heart exploded with joy and triumph, oh, I thought, oh, my conspirator, my competitor.

In her big mirror we studied ourselves, we stood side by side, our hips collided, we couldn't tell whose hips were the narrowest, eyes weren't enough, Rosa fetched a measuring tape.

My lilac panties, her white.

Angry, humiliated, exposed. Was my beautiful friend by my side. Now there was evidence for my supremacy.

The measuring tape lay on the floor, little snake of truth.

I must place my faith in my body. It gives me strength.

It's annoying only to be able to turn to others as the doll. As an image. So protected by artificiality, my whine, my phoniness. But Rosa sees me as me, she sees my struggle, because my struggle is her struggle. Is the same struggle. So I cultivate my hunger into a rose for her little fist. My sacrifice, my declaration of love, my taunt. Rosa, I'm surpassing you, I'm becoming more you than you.

Hahaha.

I think my revenge laughter rings in her dreams.

In what is far-away and grown-up.

And then I wish she'd kneel.

Worship my worship.

Surrender.

We fed her rabbit carrots in the garden. White fur, beautiful animal. It eats quickly like it's a machine of the world. We stroke. Her cage is small. Rosa wants to give her a French

fry. She had a warm little bag from McDonald's in her pocket. We'd just been. We stole balls from the ball pit. Ate the pickled cucumbers, threw the rest of the burgers out. It felt like a heart on her thigh. Freshly torn from a sheep. Warm and dead. Neither of us knew rabbits couldn't tolerate salt. Now we do. Once bitten, twice shy. Rosa's dad buried the rabbit the day after, at the end of the garden, he dug a hole just deep enough, we threw soil into it. Had made a cross of twigs, bound it with string.
Here lies Rabbit.
The rabbit's name was Rabbit.
Rosa didn't cry, she pinched her arm as we sang a bit. Pinched and pinched. Sang and sang. Rosa's dad didn't tell us off. Just stroked Rosa's hair, pulled her close.
There there, he said. You couldn't have known.

His consolation looked like a present. His consolation looked like something unknown. Rosa's dad's consolation didn't cost anything.

From an early age I understood that grown-ups were far-away planets with dark dreams. I understood that my mum and my dad had had me to feed their hatred of each other with their disappointment in me. Their daughter. Their girl from a swamp they knew nothing of. She existed, but she could never be understood.

The parents' fingers wanted to wind the child's hair around them. Poke the child in the stomach and say:

Now now.

I came from her sticky dark. Mum's.

Maybe that's why she immediately loved me and despised me so much she had to leave a mark.

Mum drove her nails into my fat baby thighs. In the photo album on the shelf, it's pink, there's a photo of me at six months, I'm smiling, I'm naked, and you can see little red half-moons.

I've come to the conclusion that these marks are my mum's handiwork.

Now I'm old enough to dodge her.
Not old enough to flee.

My bedroom is a life buoy.
All I have to cling to.

In the choppy ocean of my childhood.

I've never felt like a child. Like a stranger, yes. Like someone who doesn't belong. Like a little growth. Like something to be weeded out.

Never like the tall sunflower, admired, or like the little, delicate but lovely poppy everyone wants to pick but doesn't have the heart to hurt, they leave it be, and never like the little bluebell, blooming like ocean on the forest floor for all eyes to be lulled by.

It's my birthday. I'm tired. Mum has gone above and beyond

to make it a perfect day. Fifteen years. Mum laughs. And gives birth to my laughter. My dress is beautiful and unpleasant to bear. The necklaces on my collarbone are heavy, they look like chains. The sheet on the bed is white and tight. Like a face that wants the worst for you.

I can't bring myself to ask Mum to drive us home.

Mum has spoken of nothing but the hotel's gold-plated bathtub, the crushed gold leaf they'll sprinkle over our porridge in the morning.

I don't want any of it. Mum's clothes are stench. Mum's clothes are swamp. Her tights and panties lie on the floor, coiled around each other. Mum's naked body in the bathtub. Water sloshes over the side. Mum sings. She has a good voice. The kind of voice you can't fall asleep to. Dad said. But Mum sang me to sleep.

Once Mum has towelled off, blow-dried her hair, naked and dry she lies down on the bed. A mountain. A big, soft mum-mountain. My tears run down my cheeks. I'm beckoned for. Mum says: LIE WITH ME. And I get to be little spoon.

Riled riled riled. I am. Child child child. Mum thinks.

And like this we slide together into dreams. And like this we wake.

A fresh rose is delivered to the door. The sun shines. I'm bleeding. My period is irregular. I wasn't expecting it, not now, the bed is smeared red, Mum's thighs are red. Sara, you pig. She says, the devil in her gaze. Go get a cloth. Wash me clean. I rub Mum's skin hard with the wet cloth, ow, Mum says, careful, Mum says, and I rub more gently.

Still, I'm never obedient enough. Still, Mum says: You're being contrary, Sara.

Mum said, these blows to your buttcheeks, they're just symbolic, violence isn't violent, it's a gesture, a warning, something you should see as a finger wag, as a scene in which you play the disobedient child who must be punished and I play the woman who punishes. I don't hit you like Dad would have hit you.

I received my symbolic beating. Was consoled and consoled and consoled. Little sweetheart, Mum said, Mum says.

It's for your own good. It's to help you.

Mum loves punishment because Mum loves consolation.

I don't hit you like a father's hand would hit. A mother's violence is love. A mother's blow is just a caress exploding. A mother's love can get out of hand. It's not in cruelty. Mum strokes and strokes. And Mum brushes my hair, brushes and brushes until my hair is soft as silk. Mum kisses my hands, she gathers them in hers, and presses them to her mouth. Kisses them roughly, bites them gently, little nibbles with her teeth.

Ow, I say.

There there, Sara, Mum says.

Her clinic is called

Skin & Skin.

She's a dermatologist. She tends to old women's skin. They come to her for smooth cheeks and gossip. They tell Mum about their dead husbands, their ailments, their step-daughters, grandchildren who live far away. They have cats and dogs or memories of a fruit tree in a wonderful garden. Liane was the one who gave me the marbles. Kirstine, the paper dolls. The little tabs on the clothes that fold over the body, you have to be careful with them, not to mess it up. A little blonde girl with ringlets and blue bows, her underwear is white. I cut her out, hung her on my wall with tape, didn't give her any dresses.

She's hanging there watching over you, Mum said.

She said it in the good voice, the voice that sounded like a mother's voice. The voice I knew to be a lie but clung to all the same.

A girl went to the meadow, that was the song she sang at my bedside when I was very little, then my mother will hit me, she sang, and sang that line again, then my mother will hit me. No. I cried. No. Mum don't hit. I said. And Mum laughed.

And I aped her laughter. Nervous shadows on the wall, the dream catcher above my bed cast them.

And Mum said: If you lie to me, I'll hit you.

Then I asked her to hold my hand, and she held my hand until I fell asleep, I never noticed that she'd left the room, that the night was my own. In the living room Dad watched TV. Or he read a book.

I miss him.

He died.

The school bus ran him over. Dad was walking along looking at the sky and the clouds and at how white and beautiful they were, he was looking up, so he didn't see the bus. It was a tragic accident, in no way the bus driver's fault, the one with the thinning hair, he combed it flat over his head, not the one with the thick white hair, with the moustache, who always patted me, stroked me, my hand, when I held it out to show him my bus pass, it was the other one; he didn't have time to brake, he'd been paying attention, he said, he always did, but suddenly Dad had stepped in front of the bus, and it smashed into him and smashed him to pieces. He died on the spot. They said. They said it was painless. He was just gone. From one second to the next. A red, slimy porridge on the asphalt.

At least the bus was empty. No child witnesses.

Then it was just Mum and me.

Mum and me in the house.

A few people came to the funeral, Dario delivered his sermon, he threw soil on Dad's coffin.

It was merciful, all things considered, Dario says. A kind death. God spared him, set him free. Sara, look at me, his finger under my chin, lifts it up towards his face, he looks me in the eye, kisses me, my hair, my forehead, and then his mouth finds my mouth and his tongue breaks in. He licks my teeth.

My braces came off last year, Jette the dentist removed them. My smile is so freed now, and conniving.

I say,

STOP

And he stops at once, he looks in pain, confusion, care at me, says:

Little sweetheart. Little, poor sweetheart.

I'm with you.

I let him console me, and I feel his dick, hard beneath me. He only meant to console. He breathes on my eyes. Like God. He says. He laughs. He wants to watch a movie with me, one he thinks I'll like, understand, with my heart, that's what he says, I think your heart has already seen this movie. I think you already know it, and now we'll take in this movie together.

The Virgin Suicides.

The movie shines like a bright baby eye in his enormous TV. We sit next to each other, I've pulled my knees up to my chest, arms wrapped around my legs. I make myself as small as possible. He sits with his hands behind his neck, leaning back into the soft ocean of sofa. The warmth from his thigh is magnetic.

Can my hand be coaxed from me?

Yes.

I cough.

He smiles.

Kirsten Dunst dreams her way through images.

Wish I were her.

That smile.

I'm so in love with Dario, and Dario drinks beer from a glass, and is quiet. Quiet, apart from his breathing, hot and heavy like a marble egg in the sun on Grandma's windowsill.

Quiet, apart from the crisps he crunches between swigs of beer.

I wish beer tasted of apple juice.

Rosa is writing, my phone is vibrating on the table, I know it's her, even though she's been pretending I don't exist.

Except now I do, because my dad is gone.

Sara

it says, just that, my name. She's calling me to her.

I'm a dog.

I'm an obedient dog.

My heart is pounding.

I read the message in the rectory bathroom, I sit on the cold porcelain toilet seat and I write:

Rosa

To Rosa.

She writes:

I'm sorry.

I answer with a heart.

I turn off my phone, I don't know what I'd do if she called, if I'd take it or if I'd say where I am, at Dario's.

Rosa would make fun of me.

I piss, a long and powerful piss. I'm worried Dario can hear it hitting the water in the toilet bowl below me.

There's no more toilet paper on the roll, and no spare rolls in sight.

I drip it off. Count to ten.

I wash my hands, and the soap smells of rose. The towel is damp and yellow. The mirror is shiny, it's been polished recently, a big, red zit on my forehead blooms yellow pus, I squeeze, it explodes between my fingers, splashes onto the mirror. I consider wiping the splash away, but don't.

A nod to Dario's wife, his daughter.

They're not home right now, Dario said, when he called me.

I'm here for you, Sara. My door is always open, Sara.

We can pray for him together. Your dad's in a better place now. With God.

Come, we have all night. Come.

And the night he'd been dreaming of was the night I too had been dreaming of.

I said yes. Yes!

Now I will partake in the shared dream. Dress up and then down for Dario's and God's sins.

I rode my bike in a hurry, my nightie in my bag. In jeans. In a white crop top. Rang my bell at a dog stood drooping at the roadside, it started barking, a beautiful, black, glossy dog.

My mum's mood had imprisoned me. This was me breaking free.

I left my mum to her muted grief, she was sitting on the green sofa staring out into space, as dusk fell on her long, coarse hair and the strands of grey in it, they picked her up, gave her strength, saw the piles of washing up which stank as I snuck out the door, I'd left a note on the kitchen counter, I'm sleeping at Rosa's, it was gone when I got home, in the morning.

I rode home through the birds' morning chirping, choking tears, melancholy and glowing.

Full of longing for him.

My red cheeks were a god's.

What was that night?

I'm his angel. That's what he says.

Wings spread, legs

like a lunatic.

Kissed through, cuddled through, see-through I woke to

his heavy arm on my waist. He was breathing heavily and I was wearing my nightie, it was quite short, faded blue. I'd shaved my legs with Dad's razor from the windowsill in our bathroom. Old stubble fluttered from it, and I cried in the shower as blood trickled from the little cuts caused by my eagerness and inexperience to make my legs beautiful and ready for a man's eyes and hands.

The night was:

Dario's hand on my thigh, the warmth from it, as the movie credits rolled, he rubbed hard and harder with his thumb, it bored into my flesh, then stroked it gently.

Silk skin, he whispered, and I pretended to be asleep, my head lolling on his shoulder, my eyes closed and my breathing deep, and he said, a warm gust in my ear, I know you're awake, Sara, and carried me in to the big bed where he and his wife slept, the duvet cover was stripey and smelled of sweat. I was a warm, furry pup, the bedroom was cold, a window stood open, he took off his belt, and my chilly buttcheeks presented themselves; I got a spanking, nervous, half-hearted, quick slaps.

Ow. I said.

Oh. He said.

I was so wet and quivery.

Wet. He moaned.

Soaking wet.

With him I ceased to exist as myself, I existed as longing, light, lust. I existed as the divine child. His dreamgirl. He said. He cupped my breast in his hand. The fruit of faith. He said. And laughed.

Laughed and laughed.

Took my breast in his mouth, his dick out.

My lips quivered. It was all too much. In a wonderful way.

The little gold cross that hung on a thin leather cord from his neck, it dangled over me and was his blessing.

I could tell that the more I moaned, the more turned on he got.

His sperm shot into me as I kept my eye on the cross.

I wrapped my naked body around his. Clung to him and was safe. He found me. He understood my beauty. I was ready to love him forever because he showed me that understanding.

It's rare, that understanding.

In the morning light he peered down into his coffee, turned pale brown by whole milk from the little orangey-red milk jug I think his daughter made for him, it looked so awkward and eager, in his big hand, a bit of the rim had chipped off, and said that I was a miracle. He didn't want to let me go, crushed my hand in his when I had to rush out because his wife and daughter would be home any minute now.

I'll see you, he insisted, pushing me gently out of the door. With stressed eyes.

A black car drove past me on the deserted road, fifty metres from the house, maybe they saw me.

Maybe they thought I was beautiful.

I hate wives who look at me with sour mouths.

But I also wish they'd invite me into their living rooms and serve me little lemon cakes and juice.

Or tell me to call them, if there was anything.

At home I called Rosa. She picked up, I said hi, and she said nothing, I said hi again, then she hung up, then a message appeared:

Sorry. I wasn't alone.

Evening fell, Rosa called me back. She said she didn't know what to say. She said she missed me. And she said that I could always come to her with my grief. I know your loss, she said, do you think my mum still loves me? She asked. She said, we're eating now, Dad boiled potatoes, the frika-deller went black, I forgot to watch them, I was so afraid you wouldn't talk to me, Sara, she said, you'd be mad at me,

I know, she said, and was about to say more, I think, but I said, don't worry about it, Rosa. We're best friends. It's the two of us, I said. Against the world. Through fire and water. And Rosa said: YES. Always, she said. Always, I repeated. And she said: Yrsa was boring, she wanted to buy clothes and talk about boys, or talk about dogs, her dad is a vet and obsessed with pedigrees. Oh, I said. And Rosa said: But I gave her a friendship necklace, the one with the heart we have too, so she's going around wearing half of the silver heart, and I can't get it back. She won't admit defeat, she follows me everywhere like an idiot, I can't stand it. She won't part with the heart. Even though I've told her it no longer counts. There's no magic left in that silver.

I felt the bubbling bliss of being taken back into good graces, of reconquering Rosa, of it being me who was hers all along.

I forgive her her betrayal.

She told me to come over, sleep over at hers. Her white house with the big garden with the big, old fruit trees gave me a place to cry. The plums were yellow and beautiful. The apples on the ground small and wrinkled. We didn't dare eat them because of the worms.

My tears made Mum mad. It's no use, Sara, she said. Stop it. Now. And Mum's crying, and Mum's refusal to speak to me. Or let me go, because where are you going, Sara, she hissed from her otherwise dogged silence, and I knew she suspected that Dario had showered me with his love, and Mum wasn't stupid, Mum wasn't shocked, Mum was jealous,

Dario is a handsome man, she'd said the other day, shooting me a look, a frown, eyes prying, I crept out once she'd fallen asleep, her eyelids fluttered with dreams I hoped were good ones because then she wouldn't spare a thought for me.

My absence never alarmed her, as soon as I was out of sight she couldn't care less what happened to me, what I did, what others did to me. It was when her anger needed a target she'd go back in time and latch on to whatever crime I might have committed, her daughter, her only child, she said in a husky voice, and the wine had been drunk, and the cakes eaten. That time I fled to Rosa's house and left her behind, she said, left her to her dark thoughts, to herself, how could you, her sobbing sounded like a cough, her eyebrows were black, freshly dyed, and I just said I thought she'd be happy I'd been forgiven. Rosa had taken me back.

Mum glowered at me. I had to stroke her back in front of the TV that evening, reassure her I'd never leave her, that it was me and her against the world.

But it was, like I said, me and Rosa, against.

It was at Rosa's that I betrayed Dario. I saw Rosa's dad naked. It was an awkward moment; we both blushed. He was in the shower, he hadn't locked the door, it was night-time and I had to shit. Fuck. I blurted, and the seconds went by, I stood in the doorway, and I couldn't take my eyes off his dick, it was longer than Dario's, hung down his thigh like a shy animal, pale and skinny. A cocoon. Veins protruding under the thin, delicate skin. Rosa's dad said: Oh, and I said: Sorry, and then I slammed the door, came to my senses, stowed the sight of his muscular, glistening torso in my heart, and waited for him to have rubbed himself dry with a towel, put his boxers on, his T-shirt. He came out, blushed, mumbled goodnight, and left me.

Left me!

I was still blushing, a rose stood on the windowsill in a glass vase, it's white, the window stood ajar, the thick steam from Rosa's dad's shower was like a cheek to lay mine on. My shit was loose and watery, I'd eaten nothing, and all I had eaten was carrots. Still, it stank, I took a perfume from the cupboard and squirted it into the room and onto my throat to mask the stench.

Rosa's dad was sitting in the living room, he hadn't gone to bed, he said my name, I was about to creep past him, but he'd been waiting for me, wanted to talk to me, come, Sara, sit, he said.

I dithered. Went over to him. The floorboards creaked under me, he was serious, shy. I looked him in the eye because I didn't want to seem nervous, but he was looking down at the table, his gaze flickered, he took my hand in his without looking at me, like a dad, that's how he took my hand, and he said: I have to ask you something, Sara, I need your help. Yes. I said, tentatively. Yes?

And I thought about how my dad, when he tucked me in when I was little, put his big, heavy hand on my forehead and said: Here it's calm, here is where the sweet dreams are, little sweetheart. And he promised me he'd never leave me.

Never. He got into my narrow bed, which creaked ominously beneath us, and lay there with me until I fell asleep, then tiptoed out, and if I woke and called, he'd come in again, stay all night.

And it was so seldom he tucked me in.

Because he can't stand you. Mum said.

Rosa has become strange and distant, said Rosa's dad, she barely tells me anything, almost nothing, about her life, about her feelings. I don't know what she's thinking, I don't know how she's doing. Who she sees, apart from you, she's stopped telling me, who her friends are, if she even has any. I'm worried. About her. She's got so thin, his eyes slid over my body, and I saw a part of him take me in, my pointed breasts peeking through the airy silk of my nightie, I was taller, browner, but he didn't smile, and she barely eats, he said, and her jeans are so tight, I don't get it, and she cries a lot, she says I should mind my own business, that I'm all over her all the time, leave off, Dad, she says, and it hurts, Sara, it hurts that she no longer seems to trust me. I'm her dad. I love her. But she doesn't care. She doesn't want anything to do with me. I'm worried she's in trouble. That she's suffering. Do you know anything, Sara? Is it love? Is it unrequited love? I'll crush anything that hurts her. I won't let anyone cause her pain.

She's far too lovely.

She deserves only goodness.

I'm a terrible father.

Rosa's dad's voice was so dark and melodic, so gentle and sad. I was falling for him, maybe I'd fallen long ago, but now it stirred and made me warm and heavy, and I had no idea what to say to him.

His confessions made me squeamish. And I wanted to help. But I didn't know how to. Without betraying Rosa. Without betraying myself.

We had secrets that were important to keep. I had Dario. Mum. I had my ambition to become the thinnest and powerfullest girl in the world. Rosa had that too. And that's why we were best friends. And that's why we were arch enemies. All of this was far too complicated to bring Rosa's dad into.

Our path to supremacy makes sense only to those it makes sense to. Rosa's dad was lost.

I couldn't shed light on anything.

Why is she disappearing?

Rosa's dad didn't wait for my answer. He continued:
I looked for her diaries, I know she has one, but I didn't want to pry, didn't want to stoop so low, God no, spying on a child, my own, my angel, but despair drove me to it, I ripped the stupid little gold lock off, and then all she'd written in it were little poems that made no sense. Something about children in yellow raincoats at the beach,

a dead seagull. Diamonds and motorbikes. Has she gone mad? I think she might be sick.

I wonder if I should get her a psychologist.

He'd long since let go of my hand, but now he caught my eye, fell silent.

I said nothing, I was overwhelmed, I didn't know what to say, then I said: Sorry, I, I don't really know, he said: Hey, hey, sorry, loveliest Sara, sweet, sweet girl, it was wrong of me to make you listen to all this. I've been drinking, he pointed to the bottle of wine on the coffee table, empty, his breath was so sweet and hot,

forget about it, forget about it.

What's that perfume you're wearing? You smell like Rosa's mum, like rose! No one but her mum should smell like that, why do you smell like that? His nose was in my throat's hollow, then it was between my breasts, I didn't push him away, was embarrassed I'd brought us here, that in stealing the dead mother's perfume I'd brought him grief, roused memories.

Are you trying to lead me astray?

I can't resist your eyes, Rosa's dad says, I can't resist you, Sara, Rosa's dad says, smiling a serious smile. A smile that pains him. I can tell. That's how much I want him.

Look at your teeth, they're pearls, they could be a necklace around a princess's neck, your teeth are so beautiful you shouldn't chew with them. Leave the meat be. Don't be animal. Your smile is a jewel. Promise me you'll only ever lick and suck. You're a goddess. Sara. You don't realise how powerful you are, you don't know that the world is yours for the taking.

But I knew. I knew perfectly well.

He wanted consolation and I gave him consolation. He pressed my head down, and I took him in my mouth.

I sucked, I was a calf nursing, and he pressed himself deeper down my throat, I did my best, and it seemed to be good enough, he moaned a heavy moan, and pressed my head closer, closer to him, I couldn't breathe, then he released me, grudgingly. I gasped for air, he kissed my mouth.

Careful, I said.

He pushed into my pussy and filled it up, it was painful and good. I seized his buttcheeks and sank my nails in.

He came. Inside me. Pulled out, and I hid my face behind the cushion, didn't want to see, be seen.

Thank you. He moaned.

You should be painted. He said. That butt, those plaits. He took a picture of me.

Look here, he said, and took the cushion from me, and passed me my nightie, and poked me, and it rained. And it was a place I remembered being wonderful, in his arms, that night.

You drive me crazy.

Then he got scared, had Rosa heard? No. Quick, better get back to her room, he had crow's feet eyes, he was in a rush, and I felt a ghost watching me, a slight shiver of the curtain and a chill from a mouth I couldn't see, a sigh, the sigh of a woman who'd been his great love.

She'd seen us.

Rosa's dad didn't understand. But he looked over at the picture on the windowsill.

Rosa's mum followed me. She decided to take care of me. She decided to love me like she loved Rosa. That's what I felt, on my way up the stairs that creaked beneath me, an evil cackle. A ghost mother was my reward. Now there was care. Now there was light. White, dusty light.

I crept in to Rosa, lay down on the mattress on the floor, Rosa was asleep. I had to cough but didn't dare for fear of waking her, I couldn't bear her seeing me now, mussed, sweat wet, euphoric and gross.

I think she'll guess I've betrayed her. I'm good at lying. I said I fell when it was Mum's hand, I said at Rosa's when I was at Dario's. I tell little white lies all the time, and everyone always believes me. Angel face. But now and here, sperm running down my thighs, I couldn't not blush, couldn't not give myself away. I would come clean, and Rosa would immediately know that this night was my weapon against her. Then her hatred would come blooming back. Then her nails would be thorns. I could just about make her out, here in the dark of night, and I wished her gone so she wouldn't wake up with me, pour orange juice into my glass and ask me: Hey, Sara, what are you thinking about?

Hey?

I'd answer:

I can desire only if I know I'm desired. My desire materialises only when I'm satisfied that I'm beautiful enough for a man to direct his desire at me. As long as I remain unaware of my beauty, I'm unable to feel desire. To feel desire I must desire myself through another's eyes, the man's.
That's what makes me a thing. Makes me my own doll. And her puppeteer. I'm more than my flesh, my flaming pussy. When you run your hand over my pussy, I thrust my mound of Venus into your palm like a cat's back, I purr. It takes more than that to ignite, to bring me to climax with your hand. I'm my cold eyes taking my own measure.
How to explain it?
I'm silent for a few seconds.
I gesticulate down at the doll. My two silver bangles clink. I must study myself in the mirror, at all angles, I must know if I'm worth possessing. A girl worth owning, seeing. If I can see myself as someone a man wants to be seen with, then I can permit my desire to bloom, my blood to boil.

I make myself up, and as I watch my face taking shape, like a face of beauty, my brushes, my powder coaxing my features out, soft and lovely, I turn on, I can see that I can be looked at and enjoyed, and then I can enjoy myself, own myself, I earn the right to possess myself, and with that the right to desire. It's a right hard-won. It isn't handed to me on a silver platter. Torture myself, in order to love. I made myself up, and I got so turned on by how beautiful I'd become, the mirror my friend, that I had to take a break, after applying mascara to my lashes, it made them close, dark like the night, and lie down on my stomach in bed, and let two fingers slide into my pussy, pushing them hard and deep inside me, I'm slimy and wet, I have fingers that are too thin, nails that are too long, they're false and glittery, glued on by a nail lady called Veronica. I push a pillow under me, try to abandon myself entirely to myself, without worrying about a nail snagging, try to think of nothing and everything, big, beautiful breasts, a dick squashed between them, the movement up, down, an ejaculation, and sperm showering the breasts until they glisten, the man roars and the woman is all perfect breasts glistening shiny like fish, like cars in the rain, like feverish eyes, and the man is all roar and dick, now tired and limp and soft, little silkworm.

Or else I said:

Nothing.

Rosa's dad was nowhere to be seen. We sat eating each our half of a toasted bun as slowly as we could. The trick was to crumb so much that half of it ended up on the plate. The trick was to devour slower than the other. Rosa annoyed me.

I knew she knew we were in competition. But it was unsayable, it was all about the reward: a weightlessness to make the day possible, a superior point of departure. I wasn't the gluttonous one of us. She was. She couldn't keep it up, she gave in, and I sat with the quarter bun in hand, the thin layer of honey, sticky lips, dry mouth and a triumph as subdued as a dainty little candle flame.

She's tired. I couldn't sleep last night, she says, but she slept. It wasn't restless, either, it was the deep kind of breathing, dreams of vast, green summer forests. No detection, no terror, no suspicion. Just a heart of sleep. A daughter with a safe home. A good father. All that was Rosa's, her call: Dad, Dad.

And that it was answered.

And he comes in to us, morning, have you seen my keys? He overslept, he said, was in a hurry. Sluggish, sweet. In blue overalls, a big, flushed cheek, toothache, he said, dismissively, a sudden infection. I'd commented on it, to help, so he could glide seamlessly into our breakfast seance, so he didn't see me with his dick in my mouth, looking him in the eye as I sat there by his daughter's side, looking so young.

A child I was too. Time had hauled me into the most peculiar place where I could be anything. Where I could be Little girl/Young lady. Innocence/Trap. A warm and murky place. A nest. I enjoyed sitting there watching the shame take root in him, he looked down, didn't dare meet my gaze, or Rosa's, our eyes were stars, his swept the floor.

I had hoped he might call me sweetheart, like he called Rosa sweetheart. Bye, sweetheart, and a kiss on her hair, he hesitated, then left me.

Left me!

Fuck him.

I miss you.

Dario wrote.

I missed too, but what I didn't know.

I turned sixteen, I turned seventeen, I turned more and more obsessed with Rosa's dad. More and more tired of Dario, who never seemed to tire of me. He still called me

ANGEL.

We were on our way to school, on bikes. Mine was blue and Rosa's was red. We were a light breeze of short skirts and long hair.

My body hurt, my muscles were boiled carrots. I felt weak. Drained. Ravishing. Sweat glistened between my breasts in the sunlight.

I saw something whoosh past me, and it might have been the shadow of my future daughter. I wanted to hold on to her, examine her face, know who she was, but she was gone.

Hi, little sweetheart. Bye, little sweetheart. Until we meet again.

We had Danish and my Danish teacher was watching me with hungry eyes. Or was it just attentive?

I was the bright student. I'd understood the poem. He said. My analysis hit the mark. I'd unbuttoned my T-shirt an extra button. I felt faint as I read the poem aloud:

THE GIRLBEAST

Anew she rises toward light and wind.
A freshly made being drinking the world in,
sensitive muzzle, suckling on sin,
with young and hungry eyes, she takes amen.

My breasts jiggled in time to the poem.

Good, very good, he said, Johannes, and wrote,

GIRLBEAST

on the whiteboard.

Rosa took a bite of a pear.

The poem wouldn't let me go, it had small, stupid claws, I thought of it as a frozen strawberry in a glass of water I was soon to drink, and I was sitting close to Rosa at the little table, our arms touched, and then I felt a tap on my back, it was Peter, he wanted my attention, he wanted to whisper something in my ear.

He whispered, keen bean, and he winked at me, I blushed. His bright blue eyes were mine. A fly buzzed about my ear. Johannes came over to us, quiet, he said, a stern look at Peter, do you need help? he asked me. And he positioned himself behind me, took the pencil from my hand, had his arms around me, and went through my notes, slowly, and his breath smelled of coffee and chocolate. I so wanted to win every heart. His too, and I hoped that one day my beauty would quell his caution, his defences, his self-respect.

As he read my analysis of Piet Hein's poem, I thought this: I'm lying spread out on the teacher's desk like a petroleum-blue dress on display in all its silky glory. My skin is white like snow, like Johannes's dandruff flaking over me, like a snow, like salt. His moans are deep and good and nervous. He's heavy, moaning heavily, and lovely. Any moment now someone could open the door, catch us in the act. Him. Him, drilling into a student with his fat dick. It would be a scandal. It would be the death of him. But Johannes doesn't give a shit about his hypothetical death. All he wants is to fuck.

Are you done, I ask, my voice sharp, my voice diamond, once Johannes has spewed his sperm into me, he thought nothing of protection, he thought nothing of the condoms in the wallet in his back pocket, he thought only of the time, of my pink nipples, my fur.

Perfect, Johannes says, his cheek near mine, his beard grazing me, and he removes his hand from my shoulder, and my entire body wants to keep him there, suck him to me, but he's already headed over to Mads, oh.

When I get home I take a shower. Mum is vacuuming. She's furious and quiet. Then she explodes. Screams. Shouts. Then she turns to me, wants to console and be consoled. Wants reconciliation.

Little sweetheart, she whispers it.

I just get so scared.

Sorry. She chants.

Sorrysorrysorry.

You know I love you.

I do everything I can to make her happy again. To get some peace. Some sleep. I want to vanish into the dark and dream about dresses and Peter and the beach with the sunset that is blood-red and mine.

I will conquer the night with bright dreams. Drift among the stars like the most beautiful angel.

But Mum isn't done sobbing and demanding.

I'm spent, she's greedy.

She wants to watch *Pretty Woman*. She wants to watch it together, with me.

She doesn't want to be alone right now. She can't bear feeling so alone.

Richard Gere's eyes and Julia Roberts's legs and smile. It's Mum's paradise. It's Mum's room.

The happy ending Mum's pipe dream.

Dario is starting to annoy me. He can't give me up. He asked me to come by so we could walk his dog together, that was my invitation.

So we could talk it all over. He wrote.

Men with tentacles and wives. I love and hate them. They reach out for me and I want to be caught.

The net they cast becomes my clothes.

I don't know, Dario, I wrote.

He sent me a

?

that I left unanswered.

The next day he wrote. Come. I'm all alone here. I miss you.

I missed Dario too, but he stressed me out, and he was jealous.

He wanted to come over to mine.

It's not the best timing right now...

Sure.

Was his reply.

And my stomach hurt. Guilty conscience. I didn't know if Dario knew about me and Rosa's dad. About what was happening. But how could he? There was no way he could know. But he sees through me. My soul flickers before his gaze. Flashes. Flasher soul. He calls it. He knows me.

You can't keep things from me.

Tomorrow?

I will meet him in the hope of a great love between us. I will meet him in the dream of souls that are made for each other. I will meet him in a fierce kiss, a desire to be conquered, taken. He wants to own me, and here I am like a precious thing, a bird aquiver, a baby doll, a shard of glass to hold up to the sun.

That's what I want too.

And he replies,

yes.

He replies,

thank you.

I miss him prising apart my thighs like they were two orange segments.

I'm lying on the sofa in a T-shirt, my thighs are so glamorous, they'd love it if I were a star, if they were put on the internet, made public property.

I take a shower, the steam on the mirror afterwards, I draw a heart in it, a wry heart, a wicked one. Then I wipe it out with my palm, puff on the mirror. S.

The sun fell on the floor, in my room, a sunwarm blanket, and even my eyes feel sunwarm like it, snug and woolly, they want to swathe something, so I look at the picture of my dad on the windowsill, he smiles out from it, looking at someone, probably my mum, she took the picture, before they had me, back when they were so young, so gentle, I've never known them like that, but I can tell, by the way my dad is looking at me, at my mum, from the picture, that it was the gentle, glowing kind of love, my mum wasn't a danger back then, to Dad. She didn't snap. She didn't sob. She laughed. My mum was his beloved. They were beautiful.

They were a fairy tale.

When they went for walks in the forest she took his hand, and he squeezed hers in his. They'd pass another couple, holding hands too, and each of them thought about the others: There goes happiness.

The smiles they exchanged flew like lightning from their mouths.

Mum shone. Her smile was to drink.

She'd been a dancer when she was little, she loved to tell me about it when I was littler and still thought that my mum, that she was the most beautiful.

I miss her, the woman she was, the one Dad is looking at from the picture. Maybe she lost it while she was making me. Maybe she only exists in pictures. And I miss Dad.

His gravestone is white, I chose the little dove looking up at the sky. In loving memory.

She shouts my name from the living room, she's home. No. I whisper. And go out to her. Hi. I'm tired, I don't want to be disturbed, there's soup in the fridge, tomato, if you're hungry, this week is without end, all those faces out there, they're all out to get me. All talking behind my back. They can see I'm a mess. And they mock me for it. Sara, give me a hug, leave me alone. A bit alone. I can't take any more disruptions.

Please, whispers Dario, he's on his knees, he has his hands on my hips, his head pressed to my crotch, my skirt's smooth fabric like a shield.

He refuses to let go. You're mine.

What could happen to me. What could happen to those

I love. Love. It's too much. To bear. The dream is to be light. Give up the dark. Escape the little, skittish labyrinths.

A snowfall. A rose. I picture all that is safe. To cope.

I tell the sky: Be patient with me, make me serene.

Dario puts his hand over my mouth. I nearly scream.

My not screaming is my redemption.

Dario removes his hand, the TV hums.

Still as a potato I lie in his arms. Soon the home will break down. Soon I'll sweep it up. A smashed wine glass. A little droplet of blood.

He licks it clean. Tells me to find a plaster. But I just want him to go. I whisper it, go.

It was my finger the blood came from. My cut. I squeezed the glass too tightly when I stiffened in his arms.

He whispered down into my hair.

There there. There there.

His voice warm.

Thick and sticky like porridge.

Now he's going and I see myself in the mirror, shining

like the moon.

I take a photo of my face. My phone is a treasure trove. I have so many faces, it's my duty to immortalise them.

Pore over them.

The face from Sunday is way prettier than this face, now, there are my cheeks, red and warm. I send Sunday's perfect made-up face to Rosa's dad. And then I drink a glass of water.

My pulse slows again.

The oven shines. I poured a bag of frozen chicken thighs into a baking tray. One thigh had a head attached to it, frozen throat, frozen eyes, it was the cheapest bag at the bright blue supermarket at the crossroads. I screamed, and the thigh, or the corpse, flew to the floor, nausea was an anchor, I couldn't bring myself to pick it up again, I couldn't so much as look at it. Let it be.

Was in my room. I went in thinking I was going to faint, but I didn't faint.

The doll's house looked nice and orderly. Long ago I'd proclaimed it my one and only. A stage for the dreams I had for my future. My girlish dream. A mum a dad a daughter a chandelier a bathtub floral wallpaper idyll. Plastic apples in the little kitchen sink.
Now it was childless. It was no longer mine.
The little doll mum's doll mouth had never screamed a

scream. The little doll dad lay on the floor in the hallway. The daughter had disappeared, I think my mum vacuumed her up. An accident, Sara, it wasn't on purpose, she assured me, as I screamed inconsolably at her that she was the stupidest mum in the world.

Dario lit up my phone. He sent me a picture of his dick. My old friend. I went into the kitchen, where the chicken corpse lay in a little pool of water, it was thawing, and I photographed. And I replied with a picture of the chicken corpse.

And it was a beautiful exchange. A fitting farewell.

Said Rosa, when I told her about it.

Or she said:

There are too many beautiful girls and too many ugly men in the world. Or she said:

Sara, I don't get it, why do you pine for him, he only wants to devour you because you're a lamb, because you're a beautiful kid.
Because he has long, sharp teeth and thick, coarse fur.
Because your lips are a glazed doughnut. Your lip gloss is moonlight. Your nipples are pastel. Sweets.
Dario kills women so he can have his girls. You're a weapon. His wife dies. His dream is you because you're nothing, or a pint, here's that drink: girl dew, meadows and ruin – be angels, alight in the grass, smile, your nails are his nail scissors.

He can't be almighty without your little cold hands in his.
Without your prayer. Your kneel.
His wife will lose it.
You can't grow.
You have to stay.
Stay.
His coat is your castle. In its pockets there are mussels, his daughter collected them at the beach, receipts, for the wine he has offered you, Jesus' blood, at the bar, your legs spread in that mini.
Look, he says, with a smile like the most beautiful winter sun, pointing at a lone rose by a stile: It's Jesus, it's me.
He cuts the rose free with his penknife, hands it to you, and you prick yourself on a thorn and you both smile.
You didn't want to say ow. You don't want to suffer. You want to be what he sees.
There there. He says.
Like Mum.
There there there.
It's not because you're not beautiful, clever, aquiver. It's just so insufferable, the way you hanker after an almighty kiss on your forehead. A peace he can give you, because he's generous. A halo: because you're pure, beautiful, beautifuller, beautifullest. Darkest in the dark in dark red dresses, with pale pink dreams, wicked in mind and wicked at heart, teeth bared and panties holy, the ones he gave you. Your ponytail is his handle, pulls your head back, catches your mouth, here is kiss, here is God. Wish.

Rosa says.

Wish you'd come to your senses.

That's what she said.

And I don't tell her Dario is history. I don't tell her I'm madly in love with her dad. I've moved on. Long ago.

I've moved on, I tell her, chill, I'm in love with someone else now.

Peter?

Right!

Right! Peter!

(DAD!)

Chilled. Winter. December darkness. December frost. I can't sleep, and it's snowing. The snowflakes are heavy and falling heavily. White, wet.

Melting in the hair of the girls who are out. The girls who look over their shoulders, to see if the men who want to hurt them, if they're following, the girls who clutch keys between fingers, the little girl weapon they taught us about in self-defence at youth club, sprint or stab, gouge, tear. Keys, nails, pretend you're on the phone.

Bite.

Over to the other side of the street, does that shadow behind them follow?

Thankfully not.

Breathe a sigh of relief.

The girls walk in the snow in their coats.

The keys are for opening doors that open into hallways with shoe racks and coat hooks and hat stands. They have beanies. Boyfriends. Dogs.

They have dreams about roses in crowns in their hair as they dance around beach bonfires.

A missing utensil, the grater has vanished like dew in the sun.

The peeled raw carrots lie in wait on the plate, maybe forever. Who knows.

Sit with me a moment, said Dad to me, his stubble scratchy and knees restless. Back when I was mostly daughter. He sang this nice song about a starling. I fell asleep with my head in his lap. I woke in my bed to him making porridge. Strawberry-red eyes. He'd had a bit of wine to drink. Been just about to wake me, but then I woke.

Was late for school, no one noticed me slide into my seat, stains on my trousers.

I'm thinner now. I've been eating so little, I'm nearly not here.

It's amazing.

I'm not sick. I'm the strong one. I can do anything if I keep myself in check. If I don't succumb to my body's pleas, if I'm something other than body, something pure, something unspoiled. It's the wonderfullest, to be able to endure all the way until night falls, when I'm allowed to eat enough so I can sleep, so I can wake up, light, clear, wonderful.

The calm it gives me, the hysteria that shines from my eyes like clairvoyance: I know better. I'm able to elude.

What do you gain access to?
But what?
What do you flee?

Rosa could ask, if she wanted to:

Why do you think power is shutting your mouth? Ignoring yourself. Hurting yourself. Doing harm. What about your little heart, does it beat on three peas and a carrot? Pepsi Max. Does it work? Do you want to die, Sara? Because it's easy, it's easy to let go, just let hunger slip its slow, stupid knife into your poor heart. Anyone could do that, Sara, put a stop to it, that's no skill, you think you're special, strong. Determined. But to be honest, becoming thinner, then thinnest, that's easy. That door is open to everyone. It's not hard. You just have to feel like shit and keep your mouth shut. It's no great achievement. You're convinced it is. But it's really not hard. You see me as a loser, my dear friend, but I've risen, I'm going places, forward, up, you think control is perfection, and you think perfection is anything nearly dead. A ghostlike figure. Light steps in the snow. As if what it means to be a girl is to be a warm and quivering corpse. Be an image. You want to be an image. You want to be seen. Appreciated. Like an altar. Like art. Like you're better than the rest. Like it's easier to pick you up from the ground the closer you are to the stars. It's time to put down roots, Sara, be a tree, a rose, just? Stay in the soil, and drink. The rain is falling.

I answer Rosa's words, they plague me in the night and in sleep, they're no longer kind:

But Rosa, now you're letting common sense and fat govern, you're placing your faith in your perfect breasts and your strong thighs, in an insight you believe you've arrived at because you believe you know my path. You believe in your ability to handle anything that comes your way. That your whole life is ahead of you. A future. Of light? Laughter? Love? That you no longer have to cling to the anchor hunger is. But it's delusion to think me the loser, you have no idea, just because we seem to be standing in the same place, in front of the same mirror, it doesn't mean we see the same thing, you may deny me my victory now, but is still mine. I refute your hypothesis, that it's suicide, this, what I'm doing. That you've escaped and I'm trapped beyond help. What I'm doing isn't called anything, it has no name, but if I were to give it one, it is: show of force. Survival. Weapon. Strength of character. It is angel praxis. It is motherfucking soldier. I need wings and muscles because I'm heaven-bound, I'm redemption-bound, I'm God-bound, and I want God to fuck me. The men down here, the fathers and their saliva drool, they see me, and even though I'm pale and frail they still want me, they want the body I'm unable to possess myself, and it's so convenient and also wonderful to let them have me, I can drop my body off there, in their gazes, and their hands, and be adored as I come, and throughout it all I'm so gracious, sublime, beautiful.

Sex isn't sex. Sex is paradise.

I'm no longer dirty, I'm as white as snow.

Yrsa whispers into all of your ears: She's sick, and Yrsa's so jealous, I look fat stood next to you, she muttered, and told me to get lost.

It's not fair. Everything looks good on you, said Emma.

Only you could pull off a dress like that, said Anna.

You look supernatural, said Gry, meant it as a compliment.

I give rise to your jealousy. You won't admit to it, but it's there.

Dear choir of enemies.

Competitors. Girls everywhere pretending not to compete against each other, but oh, how they compete.

(Rosa rolls her eyes.)

I'm holy, that's what. I'm not fragile. Won't break.

The men who shower me with their love are my evidence, they hold me up to the light, because I'm glass, gold, diamond, something to find and treasure, and I twinkle back at them like this important thing.

To look at me should be like quenching a thirst.

I learned this from my mum's hatred and from the world's images. That's the school. The school isn't mine. I was born into it. To mock me for it is pure ignorance. To believe I'm succumbing to it is the stupidest.

I do what I'm told. What girls are told:

Be bright, beautiful, light. Be a sight for sore eyes, be candy. Be dreams, children, shiny pebbles. Wild flowers, shaven legs. Be dresses and hair. Be lipstick and kiss. Be daughter and doll.

Be mother and villain only behind closed doors, then you can be sure to survive in the roles available to you.

To reach, in that short skirt, up for the apple on the tree, and know what a sight it is. Cheeks peeping and poking out under the denim. To be sweet and poisonous. It makes it possible to move on. It makes it possible to let go.

You're not healthy, Rosa, you've just given up. In.

Rosa rolls her eyes again. She knows I'm waging the stupidest war in the world: the war against myself.

Rosa's truth drives me mad.

I'm sticking to mine.

I delight in the giddy hunger before the plate of bread and butter I don't eat but admire with all my heart, it smells, and I devour its smell, and am the strongest. I don't give in to the hunger, because the hunger is a castle, a place to be free. I float around it, becoming the image I want to see. A white butterfly.

Seventeen and see-through.

He likes that I'm so little.

He calls me

his little pet.

Strokes me too.

My back, hair, buttcheeks.

Would purr if I could.

I tell him. Arch my back, cat and cow, then he flips me over, wants to eat me.

Devour.

Rosa's dad's hair is big and dark.

I spread my legs for his mouth, his tongue was a slimy, fat eel thrashing into me.

You could say I was an ocean. You could say I was an idiot. You could say: angel.

Peter professed his love to me, it was at the pub after a party, after I'd said bye to Rosa, called her a taxi, she was so drunk and annoyingly beautiful, Peter watched her butt as she walked towards the car, I saw, she wobbled in stilettos and the yellow silk dress under her coat clung so tight to her hips she obeyed it like a little dog, it was her master, and they gave her looks and beers like a queen. In September, October, November Rosa had got fat and heavenly. Her breasts were enormous droplets, her thighs were strong and big; she could squeeze a man to death no problem, and he would, the gross man I've invented, die happy. I envied her, and her body made me nauseous and horny, I didn't know if I wanted to kiss her breasts, I couldn't stop looking at them. Picturing her nipples shimmering with spit. The boys were lost in her. But I knew she'd lost. Our competition persisted, but she wasn't behaving like I was its winner. She floated off at parties like an astronaut, I couldn't gloat like I'd planned to. Our dresses could no longer be the same. Hers grew and mine shrank. We threw away our shared dresses. No more loans. No more sleepovers. We slid apart.

It was no fight that flayed us apart. No evil word falling with evil intent. It was just like there was nothing to be done, we could no longer speak to each other, Rosa didn't want to be around me when I cried, she couldn't stand my whimper, that I couldn't even conjure a smile for pictures.

And I saw her dad all the time and in secret. He intoxicated me. He baked buns for me, brought them along on our forest walks. Sprinkled with sesame seeds. Bright shiny surfaces. We were never hungry enough. And we threw the buns into the stream, the birds flocked to them, hacked up the crumbs, and he ripped my dress in two when he wanted it off, I lay under the sun under the sky under him and shone with skin.

I'm so in love with you. Peter whispered it into my ear, after the kiss, he was sheepish and eager. He took my hand and said that I was. Smarter. Funner. Than. The. Other. Girls. And I could tell by the horny mist in his eyes that Rosa's butt still shone on his morning wood like a chilly moon. Which in a strange and wonderful way became a lamp that shone its light on my face, brought out the red of my lips. Cast off a hope, a dream, from her to me.
I could take him in. Now. Yes.
You're beautiful.
I didn't believe him and laughed. I didn't believe he meant it. No.
He grew confused.
Put a confused hand on my breast, under my coat it found a way, nipple perked up, it could be felt through the thin fabric, I froze.
He grabbed hold of it, a toddler's pincer grasp, my nipple a pea he was trying to pick up and smash into his child mouth, he squeezed it between his finger pulp, and it hurt, but I said nothing, I pretended the pinch was pleasure, that I was delighted that he so keenly thought I was some kind of dial to turn.
I sucked on his earlobe and discovered the little round

earring, cold taste of metal – gold. My phone vibrated in my coat pocket, little pet. I didn't pay it any attention, I was busy kissing a beautiful boy.

But its shakes had interrupted us.

It could be Rosa,
it could be Rosa's dad,
it could be Dario,
it could be Mum.

What if it was Mum? What if she'd done something terrible?

Recently she's taken to hanging over the edge of the balcony.

It was Rosa's dad, I was shiny and new with Peter's tongue in my mouth a moment ago, and dying to flee his infatuation, dying to be rescued home by Rosa's dad, so I could sit on him on a chair and slide slowly up and down, or I could let him undress me. Be bathed, washed with the soft, yellow mesh sponge that was probably Rosa's, be put to bed, tucked in, into him, fall asleep, as Rosa danced and danced and danced and sweated and sweated and locked eyes with a man who had a cute smile and green eyes and went home with him.

Rosa's dad let her go. Gave her up. But he didn't let me go. He was terrified, if we were seen together, what if, and then he was so careless, in love, proud.

Wanted to show the whole world our love, flash me about, how beautiful I was. How beautiful you are though, fuck. If I could, he said,

and knew nothing of Peter, suspected it maybe, but wouldn't pursue that kind of suspicion to its end, knew his possessive heart well enough to know that neither of us would survive the rage unleashed within him if he ever let the suspicion take root in him and turn to thought,

If I could, he said,

I'd put you on a stage and scream it for all to hear: Look at this, this diamond is mine.

The world is against us, my beloved. It's hard.

Yes, Rosa's dad, I say, in agreement, in anger at our situation – at my too young and his too old.

All disparaging eyes will shrivel. Will be shot with bullets of mother-of-pearl.

I furnish a torture chamber in my mind.

In it: a shard of glass, children never not crying. Mirrored wallpaper.

I wonder if Peter will write to me. My phone is still. Sunday is long. I go for a walk like a robot.

I walk fast, want to move on, away from myself, towards

myself, my heart is calm. I see myself through another's eyes, picture myself as a man in a car, driving past me, slowing, rolling down the window, shouting: Hey, beautiful, winking, and I see this girl, shiny and wonderful, her hips sticking out just enough to keep her skirt up.

Oh, to be that man in the car.

Be him who says:

Easy on the eyes.

Shouts:

I would,

on my way to the toilet at the petrol station.

Christian is going to dig a hole for the trampoline once the frost has passed,

flits about my ear, a moth of a sentence, brush it off. Smush it to the wall so it leaves a smudge of dark. But I heard it as I walked past a garden, a low hedge, an upright woman speaking on the phone, she looked happy. A chubby child in a balaclava and a pink snowsuit sat on the grass, reluctantly biting into an apple. I so wanted to tell that child, that daughter a secret. Tell her that a big gnarly hand could reach down through a cloud at any moment, and with the leftovers of the cloud, like soap bubbles on skin, the hand will curl around you, little girl, and squeeze you, and pluck you from the ground, pull you close, and let you snuggle into its soft whiteness, and the sunlight will shut your eyes, and you'll never see your mum, your dad, again. All you have to do is lie there and light up with light. God won't save you. He didn't save me. God will love you. Desire you. Play with you. Such a lonely castle it is to be sublime. A castle made of gold and diamonds and tears. A castle to turn you into a real princess, a castle to give you power and pain. The pain isn't unbearable, you can live with it. You learn to. I know that this floor, it's scrubbed with your tears, that your maid will collect them in a bucket, wring a rough cloth over the salt water, and wash and wash as if her life depended on it, which it does, because God is Dad and Dad is God and Dad and God aren't about to tempt fate, aren't about to let their daughter, their girl, languish in impure rooms. All will shine on you like your golden hair in the sun's summer light, little hide. And there the girl sits in the garden, maybe her name is Ida, never to be initiated into this secret, I'm incapable of luring her in, even as I lack a successor, even as I seek someone to confide in. The little girl will become a big girl will become someone other than me. Herself. Will become happy. There's nothing I can do. Can't reach her. Can't make her mine. Can only let her stay in the garden with her happy mum. With her bright future. Her milk teeth, milkweed. Trampoline hole.

She isn't my daughter.

Oh:

Evening:

Sara, yesterday was amazing, see you tomorrow.

Peter wrote.

Joy and terror.

And in the morning, a snowy Monday, I'm aquiver. I make myself up, primer, foundation, mineral powder, dash of rice powder, highlighter, rouge, eye shadow, eyeliner, mascara, lip gloss.

Brush my brows bushier with a toothbrush.

Ready myself for war.

For Geography and break time, for evil eyes and gossip girls behind me.

For stench of morning breath.

The hunger that carries me through it all unscathed. My determination paying off. I'm afloat. I'm barely touching the floor.

Johannes asks me to stay behind after class, wants to praise me for my talent, did you really write this yourself?

Blushing.

I'd showed him a poem I'd written.

Boys.

Mum buys me what I want, that's how she cares now,

she likes seeing me made up.

Doll.

She calls me, when there's life in her eyes. When I'm nice. A hand around my neck.

She's stopped being so mad, so snappy, she cries a lot, sleeps a lot.

Stinks.

She won't shower.

Or brush her hair.

Get money.

From Mum.

From Rosa's dad.

When I ask for money.

They want what's best for me, both of them, they assure me.

Mum sickens me. I don't want her face haunting mine.

Rosa's dad prefers my face naked. He takes my face in his rough hands, Rosa's dad is a builder, dreamed of becoming a musician, a star, the stages are still waiting for him, there's a guitar up in the attic, with rose stickers on it, he met Rosa's mum, wanted to love and provide, and houses are beautiful, mortar is beautiful, he says, kisses me on the forehead, says, wash your eyes, and I use Rosa's makeup remover, it's on a glass shelf in their bathroom, the tiles are grey and clean, there's underfloor heating, expensive towels, the soft cotton pads are gentle on my skin, I dab and dab, pulling the black from my eyeliner down my cheeks, it won't all come off, have to take a shower.

I step out and am passed a towel. Rosa's dad looks at me and looks serious, looks horny and ashamed of himself.

You know well, I know well, that this, this, it can't go on.

He wrings his hands, his eyes resting on my breasts.

My breasts are dripping. My long hair is dripping, a little pool at my feet.

I don't know if he was expecting tears, acceptance, me to believe him, I don't. I know he's only saying it to redeem himself. I can tell he's trying to convince himself that he's looking after me. But he doesn't look after me. He loves me. Wants to fuck me. To pieces.

He can't hide it.

I have him. His heart is mine. His dick is. His care and his respect.

He is mine because I am his.

He sees a bright light in me, sees my future, that I'll do great things.

I'll become a wonderful thing.

You already are.

Wonderful.

Saviour.

He looks at me in admiration. In gratitude.

It's like I'm addicted to his praise, his deification.

It's only happened once that he called me

Rosa.

Rosa,

after a long, warm kiss, his lips still tingling with it, his hand was around my neck, the tip of his nose touching the tip of mine, and her name in his mouth,

we both froze for a moment, then we pretended like nothing happened, carried on kissing. And I jumped up onto him, wrapped my legs around his waist, he held me there as the kiss continued.

He throws me onto the bed, I fall like a soft, heavy pillow. And close my eyes as he, his hands on my knees, pushes my legs apart, at first I resist, a little, to heighten the suspense, strong thighs, he croaks, then I give in.

I began to hate Rosa. Hate her for her ability to appear above it all. I grew more and more nervous she suspected something, but if she did she pretended not to, let it happen. What was happening.

Shrugged her shoulders, couldn't be bothered to let it bother her. She wasn't hostile but she was no longer mine. That much was clear. She sat next to Yrsa now, Yrsa the millpond, Yrsa the handball player, Yrsa the tightlipped. She didn't get me to accompany her to the toilet, she didn't invite me over to hers.

Hers that felt like mine now. Like I was its secret.

Rosa, she'd gotten so hot, so hideous. Vulgar and stuck-up. She'd forgotten me, forgotten our dream of becoming nothing together.

I was to blame. I was the one who betrayed her.

I wanted to usurp her. It was all on purpose, I would become her.

It was cruel of her to launch herself into something she knew I had no desire to be. An avoidance tactic, a way to give me the slip, I reached out and all my hand closed around was air.

But I could stand where she'd stood, I could possess what

she'd possessed. The little, dainty dresses, she'd said so herself, just take them, and I took them.

I took her mum's beauty, her dad's attention.

Dario was just my warm-up. He's paled now. I know he prays for me, every night, masturbates to the thought of me, post-prayer, every night, after he's squirted sperm into an old sock, he sends me a heart, or a picture, or an I miss you.

Asks for pictures of my naked feet. Remembers how well they worked on his dick.

You're a little monkey, little sweetheart.

He said.

And I think he hopes and waits for an answer. He keeps at it. I keep my silence. I don't know who will cave first. I'm not afraid of him, just a bit. I don't miss him, just a bit.

Rosa's dad has forbidden me to have anything to do with Dario. He's sick. He says. A pig, he says. And he strokes my hair, and he places a coke on the table, opens it, and sighs.

Brings out the dreamcake, begs me to eat.

I give in to the smell of coconut and sugar.

Rosa's dad is the one my world revolves around. Now. He is my God. I can only have one God. I can only handle one smitten man at a time.

My dad used to make me rye porridge in the mornings, he used to plait my hair. When a man gets a daughter he learns how to plait, Mum insisted, and he practised with string, with Mum's hair.

Before I came to the world.

At night I heard the car's engine start, he drove off and I don't know why. He came home the morning after, and he smiled at me, had bought me a present, some sweets, looked tired, do your homework, he'd tell me, not to disturb him. My mum went around with red eyes and demanded explanations from me about things I could hardly explain: Why are you so rude? What are you looking at me like that for? Do you think you're a princess? Untouchable? Why did you steal my jumper? Tell me where it is. Now.

Little brat.

Then she went in to rest.

I made bead pictures, which Dad, taking great care, ironed for me. A pink heart, a black square. The smell the half-melted beads emitted was hypnotic. We kept them in a box I'd decorated with feathers and glitter.

My secret shrine.

Dad was full of admiration.

You're a brave girl, Sara, he said to me the day I'd climbed high up a tree to where a cat was crying, it couldn't get down, I got it down, got a scratch on my arm, it bled. The cat wriggled from my arms and shot off, it made me sad, I wanted to hold it close, look after it, but it probably belongs to another little girl, said Dad, and he said: Mum doesn't like cats.

Mum shouted from the living room.

I hate cats.

Dad became Dario became Rosa's dad.

Rosa's dad became my salvation.

Here in his kitchen I warm my hands around a cup of rose-hip tea. Here in his kitchen I keep quiet as he hums as he fries an egg for himself. The radio is on, and I don't hear words, I only hear breathing, when the person talking takes a quick breath to sustain their torrent of speech, then a woman says:

We're keen to bring in the kind of people the future needs. The future starts tomorrow.

Rosa's dad hears nothing, and his beard tickles my cheek during a kiss.

I'm kissing. I write to Dario, who asked:

What are you doing?

I'm tired like a big, dark bush. Pissed on by the same old

dog every morning and evening for a thousand years.

I could kneel for her in front of my mirror and be scrutinised by her eyes.

Her eyes have taken up residence in my eye sockets.

Her eyes took me. She's called anorexia, in my record, when I talk to the psychologist.

I call her

beauty. Purity.

Power.

The psychologist is called Jacob. He doesn't say much, looks at me a lot. I'm here against my will, I tell him, the first time I'm at his, in his practice. I'm here because other people think I should be. To keep the peace. A short, pale hair lies on the sleeve of his black jacket. He has a dog. A poodle.

No, a labrador.

He has a summer house.

He likes watching movies.

Like you.

He says.

He recommends movies to me.

Watch *Repulsion*!

Watch *Possession*!

Thanks, Jacob. I say.

You understand me.

I mean it.

He's tall. Dark hair.

His glasses are round and big like breasts.

I'm not going to tell you anything. I tell him.

Jacob nods.

He's forgotten to zip up his fly.

I've worn a tight black dress. I bought milk on my way here, which I didn't manage to drink in time, which is lying in my bag turning sour while I cry courageously, while Jacob looks at me expectantly, the words that don't come out of my mouth lie in a little tulip in a blue vase at my daughter's christening.

Silence suits you. Jacob says. We can stay silent forever. Jacob says.

If that's what you need.

An hour with him costs 1,000 kroner.

Money well spent, says Rosa's dad.

I tell Rosa's dad the psychologist is called Anna.

To keep the peace.

My little white fur protects me.

To protect me my body has grown tiny, fine hairs, to compensate for fat, I'm an animal.

A very hungry girl.

I want to rip.

I tell Jacob I don't think it's fair that he's getting paid for my silence.

I hope Jacob thinks I'm beautiful.

I hope he wants to stroke my silky back.

Peter wants nothing to do with me. Won't look at me. He sees through me. Sees the other girls, sees Rosa. Sees Frederik begging Johannes for a deadline extension.

Nothing to be done, says Johannes, kind and cruel.

Anyone else? And I can see a tear on Frederik's cheek. Frederik has 60,000 followers. He's a model. He's the mayor's son. You're so beautiful, I told him at a party, even though I couldn't stand his dad, and even though I didn't want to fish for his attention, except I did, because those little puzzled wrinkles he gets between his eyebrows when he's thinking, when Johannes asks: When did women in Denmark get the right to vote, and he doesn't know when and he can't bear not knowing, they're icing and church bells, and he turned away, beer foam on his upper lip.

And I retreated to the toilet in the cellar, where I cried, where Yrsa came in as I was coming out, and I saw the smile that carried her through the rest of the party like a sleepy elephant and all the way home to bed, where she must have thought:

I'm the winner.

I picture her as a grasshopper, and myself calmly snapping off her head and eating her body.

Rosa wants to be Peter's girlfriend. I no longer exist. Slut is whispered in the nooks and crannies. Slut is written on my locker in red nail varnish.

PRINCESS.

Rumour has it I'm fucking Johannes because how else would I get such good grades when I never say anything in class.

I receive a handwritten letter on squared paper, it's Eva from the other class, with the beautiful hair and the beautiful body and the ugly face (waste of hair and body, whispered Rosa in my ear once, back when I was in her orbit), who, in solidarity with my situation, she wrote, just wanted to let me know that she too had taken a sugar daddy.

Where else do you think my Chanel dresses come from? My white leather bag.

I'm on your side.

She drew a heart next to her name. Her number.

I could kill.

Or die.

Could I go to the cinema with her? Hang out in the shopping centre afterwards? Drift? See a dress and another and get our belly buttons pierced? Blue and white stones. Paint our nails. Take pictures in underwear. Borrow one of her books.

Eva, I'm not you.

Stay away from me.

I cry a little, my tears drip down onto the outstretched hand the letter is.

Then comes Rosa, she's a flitting butterfly, frantic and

forgiving, for the briefest moment. Peter loves her, he said so, and she feels sorry for me. She sees my red cheeks, my crying, she gushes down next to me in a green suit and straightens out my hair. She opens her arms to me, says: Come here, and I fall into her, and her warmth, then she holds me a bit, lets go, says, as lunchtime ebbs:

It's like Dad thinks you're a hole to fall into. Like a teenage girl is something to be wary of. A man really ought to watch out when he reaches the age when he has a house, job, wife, child, a life it would be unbearable to lose. A hedge to be trimmed, a bill to be paid.

But then it happens.

It's impossible to resist, that little, scampering girlbeast's power. She seems oblivious to the magnetism of her butt. Those jeans, like they were painted on.

What does she know? This girl, who is you, Sara, and me. His own daughter. Does she know that about her jeans? About her breasts? About her way in the world, that it's as bait?

But it doesn't stop him, that you could be me, that I am you, from feeling betrayed.

Because the care that blooms when this hair spreads itself over the pillow next to him, a night he's been called on to watch over, like the grown-up he is. When she lies sick, is a student, a daughter's friend, a babysitter, a gymnast, a foster child.

The care that blooms so beautifully and nobly. Now it beckons him down paths he never in his wildest dreams thought he would tread, because he wants to foster, he wants to look after, take care of, stroke, embrace.

Then suddenly he wants to fuck.

What's up with that!
But no, it's not even that he wants to, he is fucked, it's done to him, poor thing. He is fucked by an almost-child, a queen before her coronation, a bamboo shoot, a kitten. And he is her victim, this he knows, about this there reigns no doubt in his pure heart.
But he's shocked. He has no idea how it happened that he happened to fall into this trap. The girltrap.
It exists. It does.
That kind of conduct, Sara, we know all about it. We are the holes a good man can fall into. The very misstep.
Never again will he find his footing. Now he is outcast. Now he is convicted. If not by law, then by the world.
And the dangerous thing about us is that we know it all too well, we know what we are, Sara, the two of us, but we feign not knowing.
They whisper to each other, these poor men, in their locker rooms, in their open-plan offices, on their golf courses:
She's a sweetheart, that girl, teetering about our hearts like a famished mosquito, a drowsy fly, with her beautiful friends she's beautifuller than. She knows she has the power to make blood boil, and us crack. Bring us to our knees. She need not do a thing, but whatever she does do could be fatal. She will ruin us.
Watch out.
But then they don't watch out. Because their dicks rise up, gallant as they are, when we pass them by, with our ripe faces, our open mouths, warm tongues and big dreams. Our entire futures lie bare before us, and our skin clings to our fat like salmon skin. We are playful and greedy. Intoxicated and bewildered. We are a force of nature they can't evade.
They must and will send us a picture of their erect members.

It is the fault of our siren song, Sara. Those pictures, they are the tit for our tat.
Say thank you for the dick.
We asked for it.
My dad said to me, when I confronted him, said I knew you were screwing, that's how I ended up wording it, Sara, it's unbearable that you left it to me to say it, but, well, I have to bear it, like I bear so many things, like I bear my mum's death. He said: Rosa, what is there to say, it's like Sara's existence, the fact of Sara, is a gulf that just opened and opened itself to me, I don't know how it happened, but it happened, but I'm not proud of it, I'm not, believe me, Rosa, and he looked genuinely confused, like it pained him that he of all people should find himself in this kind of trouble. But then I saw him looking at you through the windscreen, and the desire emanating from him, shame a mere shadow cast on the wall.
He was an ugly lamp in my childhood home, and I couldn't stand that he was my dad.
I just wanted to turn him off. Do you see, Sara? I didn't want Dad to be him, that man.

Dad is supposed to be Dad.

Do you remember that time at the disco, Sara, we were visiting Randi, my cousin, and we let ourselves get drunk behind the bushes by the church, and someone from year 12 was sniffing lighter fluid and told us to kiss, and we did, to the audience's delight, to the boys', and we took off our panties, and donated them to them, and they were jubilant, and bewildered, and then one of them scrunched both pairs in his hand, and later they were in the back pocket of his jeans, and Randi went out to smoke, said we were gross, and we could tell she was jealous, Axel BB offered us a lift to town, only a bit drunk. We were headed for Shooters, where CC tried to push one of his petrol fingers up me. Under the table. I was wearing that denim miniskirt, with the back pockets, which was actually Randi's and was too big, it kept almost sliding down. Your butt crack is showing, that was Randi's gleeful shout, and she felt better about herself because her item of clothing had betrayed me, but worse about herself because my butt made me look so good in the moonlit dark. She forced a pizza slice into me, from Peach Pit, beef and sour cream dressing that ran down my chin, onto my clothes, and in spite of everything held my hair while I threw up. Nik & Jay sang.

A night owl whistled at us, and we mooned.

Jessica's dad is a wolf, said Randi, everyone knows that. He's only a night owl because he loves to ogle.

She's still serving big soft serves to Germans at the Tourist Grill. Rot Wurst oder Bratwurst? she says in our nightmares. The pickled cucumbers glazing her eyes like contact lenses.

I remember, Rosa.

You had sex with a surfer.

Rosa nodded solemnly.

June nights and exams drove me to despair. Rosa's words and Rosa's dad's kisses. I was consumed. But I passed everything with flying colours. Last exam was social studies, I had to outline the Danish labour market model, the censor drank three cans of coke, and he smiled encouragingly every time I hesitated. A gold cross lay between my breasts and wallowed in sweat. I came out of the room and whispered: A*, to Mum, who smelled of red wine and the roses she held in her arms, a giant bouquet, she was the only one waiting for me, I snapped at her when she tried to put the student's cap on my sweaty hair, snatched it from her and put it on myself. She needed to pee, so I stood abandoned and dull with all those roses, making myself as small as possible. A thorn tore my arm bloody, and I got some on my dress. A modest cheer came from further down the corridor, it was Rosa's dad and Yrsa and Peter, they greeted Rosa as she emerged like a gold sun and said: A*. And her dad embraced her, and Peter embraced her, and Yrsa embraced her. I gave a tentative wave, but she didn't see me, but her dad saw me and thought the wave was meant for him, and he held a finger to his big, red mouth, shh. Turned away from me and led the little party in the opposite direction of me and my loneliness. Mum came back, placed a hand on my shoulder, I allowed it, and said: I'm very proud of you, Sara. Her eyes were shiny. She was out of breath from the stairs. She wanted to find a place to sit with me, with the champagne glasses, we'll make a toast to you, sweetheart, but I just want to go home, Mum, now, I said. On the way to the car I had to let her arm hang around my shoulder like a proud and happy mother's arm to prevent her from staggering in her high heels on the gravel, drunk and nervous as she was, her gait shaky and revealing. If Rosa saw her she would have seen the empty bottles hidden in the bottom drawer in the kitchen.

I held my head high beneath my cap as I guided her to the car.

Mum was nice, she understood me. She didn't care for all that fuss either, she said, behind the wheel, meaning the ceremony and its afterparties. Celebrations. Threatening me with their light and laughter. Consolation streamed from her, and she said we could drive by a jewellery shop for a silver heart.

I got it and still have it.

When Mum had fallen asleep, I rode my bike to Rosa's dad's house, Rosa was out celebrating, sleeping at a friend's, he said. His shirt was black, and I could see the imprint of her powder on the collar.

Congratulations, sweetheart, he said with pride in his voice and buried his face in my hair.

It smells of poisonous green apples.

We ate the leftovers of Rosa's graduation cake.

He tells me to keep my student's cap on while I ride him to climax.

You fuck me so well.

I wish you were a movie, he whispers.

I could like him.

I think.

Maybe love?

Maybe forever.

In spite of the ugly teeth.

Rosa.

The gold frame around the mirror in the hall above the dark, slim écritoire in which Rosa's sunglasses, scarves and nail varnish are kept wants to kidnap me, possess my face and wish for it that it was a painting. That would be the most merciful.

Be on display, a decoration in his home, still hanging there, worthy and mysterious, long after his death.

We'll get married! he says.

What about Rosa, what about Mum, what about people?

Fuck everyone, Rosa's dad says, and he means his proposal with a force that takes even him by surprise.

He senses the young men lurking in the wings, he knows that my hand might be seized, by anyone, that I'm a girl with a greedy and easily charmed heart.

That I want to leave it all behind.

Be driven away in a red car.

That I'm tired.

Afraid.

Say yes.

Yes.

I say.

He kisses me on the tip of my nose.

The engagement ring will be of gold. Shiny as eyes. Eternal as death.

The date is engraved. May you never forget this day, my beauty, he says, has his hands on my hips, blows out the words.

I love you.

He doesn't need to marry you. He really doesn't, is what Mum said to me, implored.

She'd taken my hand in hers, and my hand lay there shaking in hatred, my palm sweat glazed it and turned it into a little piglet farrowed by a sow, when she let go.

I think he'll come to regret it, so promise me you won't be sad, sweetheart, when he leaves you.

I hold my tongue.

The wedding is set for 5 June. The day after my eighteenth birthday. I've had a dress sewn by a seamstress, it's a perfect fit, like a cast. It's white, it's a cloud. I drift towards Rosa's dad, who's stood there like a flagpole.

There aren't many guests. The guests are glittery like fish. Hungry like bears after winter hibernation.

Most of the guests are men, most of the women we know have turned their backs on us.

Those beautiful backs in backless dresses.

They have other parties to attend.

Our party still exists.

We've hired a photographer. We'll always remember us. As we are now. Bound for each other.

I am young and beautiful and my future lies ahead of me. He is proud. Shameful and horny and fatherlike. Take care. Until death do us part.

I'll take care of you, he whispers, every night, before sleep takes me. I believe him. A rock, a hope, arms.

Mum perches nervously on her pew in yellow, her handbag in her lap, her hands wringing as we sing.

We sing about love.

The church is decorated. It's white flowers, pearl garlands around necks. The decoration is me too. I glide forth like light itself. To the altar, to the man, to surrender.

The priest who marries us is called Stacy.

Rosa has gone to Paris to be an au pair in a millionaire's house. She sends a bouquet with a card. Good luck. It says. You deserve each other.

The thorns haven't been cut from the stems, they're red, the roses.

I am wed.

I am Rosa's dad's wife.

Do you want to know his name?

Guess.

I won't give it all away.

Wrest it from me, if you must own everything.

A little twitch by my left eye.

Then we walk hand in hand to the party. He and I. Crushing each other's. Rings shining rose gold on our fingers.

Confirming the vow: forever yours.

I cry three tears:

Mourning.
Joy.
Fury.

I walk through the party as if it were a fever. An unpleasant thing soon to pass. Still my cheeks burn with a peculiar force. Ethereal red porcelain doll cheeks. Everything is painted on. My future too. My eyes shine like the stars Rosa's dad likes to point out to me. I've become a wife.

The Plough can't be fled to. The Milky Way isn't a way. Alas.

Horses graze in my nightmare in my hometown. They are headed to the forest to ride with the girls who look after them in the stable. Riding boots knock against flanks. Small, slender arms and legs kick and hit. Full speed through the green foliage, the dream that is a summer forest, whip at the ready. Helmets are tossed onto beds when the girls return home, smelling of horse and sweat.

My veil lies in disarray on the floor in our hallway.

It was torn off me in euphoria.

I sit at the table and reach for my glass which is full to the brim with red wine, an uneasy hand poured it, a hand rests on my shoulder. It's an uncle's. Rosa's dad's. His dad is here too. It's the first time I've met him. He's weak. Sick. Has dressed in a red tie, red socks. Green velour jacket. He's in good spirits, makes a speech. Calls my appearance majestic. Calls me sweet like chocolate. To think, he says, looking down at his son, looking at me, that you were capable of reeling that in, an adorable creature.

He says CHEERS.

More uncles kiss my cheeks.

All the guests seem to be uncles. One of them kisses my mouth. I want to keep kissing him. I'm dizzy with alcohol and hunger. All I eat of the wedding cake is the bite Rosa's dad feeds me. A little mouthful from the fork, it glides down like a forest slug.

It's still crawling around my stomach to this day.

The wedding night is a fog. I'm drunk. Rosa's dad rips my party dress to pieces. He's more drunk. An uncle wipes his butt with the veil, he looks apologetically at my mum when she barges into the toilet to have her suspicion confirmed, she'd seen him staggering about, laughing like a mechanical elf, in search of something to spoil, I can spot destructive eyes like those from a mile off, is what she says to me, after having bitten him in the bicep and thrown him out. But he refuses to leave and spends the night crooning in the garden in the dark, as I, for God knows what time, am Rosa's dad's paradise in a bed in the dark in his arms.

The wedding night is a flower meadow. I spread all I have

for him. Rile him up with a heart-shaped hole in my panties.

Buttercups sparkle in the green. $$$.

And soon I am hell. My tongue licks like flames.

I weigh his silky soft balls in my hand, and feel like squeezing them, hard, like they are plums, the juice could run from them.

My gums are bleeding a bit, my knees.

Soon I'll be joy itself.

There are sweets in the glovebox, more where that came from, he says, indicating. We exit the motorway, and the country road leads us to a small, modest cottage. Thatched. Formerly a dead person's, it was cheap. Your new home, says my husband, Rosa's dad, picking me up and carrying me over the doorstep.

The chimney is just for show. Once it was important.

I can hear the cows singing.

Mooooooooooo.

Shhh.

A finger over my lips.

The wheat is golden and the breeze makes it dance.

What's that? The nasty brown stuff?

Flypaper.

But the flies fly clear. Eat cowpats and buzz merrily about.

All the moths we'll never get the better of. Just when there are close to none, there are a couple more we must have missed.

Rosa's dad works out how to turn on the TV. Then the light and images roll. Then we kiss on the tatty sofa soon to be thrown out.

We'll get a new one, he says, sky blue and soft as butter.

Sometimes I cry a bit in the bus shelter, there's almost never anyone else there.

Most people have cars, here.

One day, as the tears roll quietly from my eyes, as a cloud-burst comes to an end and I'm standing there in my release, a boy surprises me, he seeks shelter from the rain, he says, doesn't have an umbrella, is soaked through, and he asks me if I want a biscuit? He has an entire packet of rich teas in his schoolbag, I say yes please, and he hands me two, I show him I can flip them in my mouth, he's impressed, and asks me what I'm going to do when I get home?

Toast buns, I think, I say.

And watch movies?

Yeah!

I'm going to do that too.

When it's raining, and I've been to school, and I'm sad, I'm allowed to watch two movies, in a row! If I want, my mum says, the boy says. My favourite movie is *Snow White*. My name is Jens.

Sara, I say.

2037

I'm thirty.

I find myself in a room. I'm renting the room from Monika. She took pity on me, because she has faith and sees the faith in me, in the way I look up at the sky, she says, and because she thinks I'm gorgeous, and because she gets to peep through the keyhole when I'm in the shower.

My bed is hard and narrow. But nice to look at. My view is incredible, I part the gossamer curtains and look out onto the loveliest park, a nude, marble woman stands with her back straight and hair long and everything perky in the middle of a fountain. I'd be happy if I were her.

A sparrow has settled on her head. In her nest in the tree by my window her three eggs await the warmth of her feathers.

My landlady is rich and frugal.

I get dresses and food.

I eat one meal a day, dinner, which I eat greedily and anxiously. A fried egg, a sausage, tomato soup.

I'm free to do as I please. I read novels, poems. I sleep. The news in the papers and on the TV wears me out. Everything is falling apart.

I'm a ghost now. I kidnapped myself before insanity kidnapped me. A wise move. But not an easy one. You mustn't think that. You who watch my back and are so keen to pass judgement. I despise you! You want to pick me apart to iron out your own little pain. Nothing is a tablecloth. Not even pain. If you're sick in the head then consult psychiatrists. There is so much perfect medicine available. Take it.

Leave me in peace. Peace is all I ask for. And deification. And pedestals.

Let me be heavenly, heathen. Insufferable.

I left behind the little I knew, it wasn't much, it wasn't loving, I haven't lost anything.
If I returnd, it would be only to haunt.

My heart was dead freight, I cast it from me so I could ascend into thin air, I seek the angels now. Sublimity, loneliness, rest.

I don't pray to God, don't pray for forgiveness, but I masturbate to the thought of Dario turning to all-consuming fire when he comes anywhere near my body. When I am a girlchild.
Wonder if he still fishes for confirmands.
Wonder if his wife found the panties I left in her underwear drawer. She probably wrote them off as her daughter's. Yellow, ruffled, dirty. His favourites.

I watch girls of 13 14 15 16 17 sunbathing by the fountain, they lie on their stomachs, backs, they're in shorts, wrap dresses, playsuits, crop tops, skirts, tank tops, T-shirts, dresses, just underwear, jeans, shirts. Sweaters, if a cloud moves to block the sun. They have ponytails, claw clips, bobs, long, flitting locks, fringes, centre partings.

I was them. I hate them. When I see them I see loss.

I want to be their friend. Their confidante. Their queen.

They should crown me.

But here I am behind the curtain, and am a witch, a secret, a sad story. A grown-up. A mourner.

My laughter is braying, my hands are haggard and my hands want to pull the girls' hair. Flay the small, round, sparkling gold earrings from their small, lazy earlobes. Those ears, they think they can get away with anything. Fuck you and your small, strokeable girlears, small girlchildren. Soon enough they'll bleed blood onto pillows that belong to men who want the best and the worst for you.

Soon enough the stains from your assorted bodily fluids will alert the wives. The wives will hate you, not the men. The men they'll merely condemn. Hate is for girls. It's so dulcet, so easy to hate a girl. Especially if she's beautiful. Especially if she's powerful.
You girls will never meet the respect you deserve.

At best you'll be taken pity on.
Called victims.

When it comes to survival, you do what you have to do.
When you fall in love, you fall in love.
If you don't have a home, a home must be found.

I buy books, I leave the books by the fountain, hope the

girls will consider them presents, take them home in their bags and read them, because girls have inquisitive minds, this I know. Their puffed sleeves and asphalt kisses ooze ambition, audacity. They want to know what life is. What death is. What love is. I've chosen the titles with care.
I've made a school, appointed them my students.
Their roller skates lie in the grass missing their feet. Their sandals sigh in exhaustion.
Painted toes, they shine red like apples.
I leave short dresses wrapped in tissue paper, I have the money, and on the internet I can find everything the heart desires. The heart desires dresses made of fabric so light you can barely tell you're wearing them. My heart desires to see these short dresses on these girl bodies. Nipples peeping cautiously through fabric. My little paper dolls below are sceptical. But word spreads, and more and more girls flock to the fountain, hysterical and eager, they want presents; when the first of them has dared to crawl into a dress, a sunshine yellow one, the next follows, canary green, the next, sky blue, and the next, lavender, and the next, postbox red. They crawl and crawl. In and in. To the dresses. My heaven below. They dance around, like a rainbow, bathing in the fountain, splashing each other with water. Braying keenly. Knock knees, corkscrew curls, ankle socks. I can almost taste them.

My landlady knocks. Do I want a macaroon slice? She baked them herself. I don't dare decline, so I sit in her kitchen at the round, rickety table and bite my way through the porous cake. It dusts my lap like fine snow. I brush the macaroon snow off me before rising to strike the back of her head with a hammer. Still, I'm shocked by how easy it is,

her skull breaks instantly, her shining hair coloured red by blood. She falls, Monika. The nausea only hits once I'm back in my room. I throw up. Wash my hands. It was an impulse murder. The hammer I'd had in my hand baggage. Ready for enemies yet to come.
Or if the past were to seek me out.

But no, it's not true, I'm lying again, sorry. Of course I'm no murderer. I'm too refined for that. Too squeamish more like. I can't bear the thought of blood, let alone the sight. Monika is very much alive, right now I can hear her fussing with the washing up, humming as she does so, a lullaby, and I don't want to know what or who is to be sung to sleep, and I think her good mood is because I for once ate up. The slices sit heavy in my stomach and make me cranky and vengeful. The last thing I want to be is fat. But Monika misses my breasts. Here in the room are only the living; me and the plant, its green leaves stretch towards the light from the window.

It's true about the hammer, though, I keep it on me. Mostly as a souvenir. I'd rather do away with it, it unsettles my soul, dredges up glass shards and tears.

A painful jolt of the heart. Here in Monika's house. Here in the room. Here with the curtains and the bed and the tree outside, with the flower in the vase. With the wardrobes and the shelves and the bookcases and the stools and the pillows and the shadows.

No doubt the furniture wonders what will become of me.

Some sweets in a bowl on the table, they're acid green and boiled, they're beautiful, I loathe them. I don't have the patience to suck until they dissolve, and I hate to crush them to bits between my teeth. Wish those sweets were coins, wish there was a shop where they were legal tender. I could buy my way to absolution.

Put an end to Rosa's dad and his sordid soul.

He died such a lovely death. In my imagination. Poisoned and unaware of misdeed or deed or death itself. Hope the devil gets him. He does. Now the flesh is torn from the bones. Firebirds devour him in the stifling dark below. He is forever in harm's way. My beautiful beloved wretch.

It's so cool here now the sun has retired like the sleepy aunt it is. The evening brings me a blanket of calm. I lie under it and wet it with sweat, tears and piss. Tomorrow, Monika will come and wash it.

She doesn't speak of my condition, I look more and more unkempt, I think I'm sick, she smacks a big, lazy hand onto my forehead, it lies there like a fat starfish, warming to the fever, she asks if she should help me into the bath? Come and wash me clean with a sponge? I nod, and the way she washes me is soft and lovely. I'm laid in bed. Tucked in. And the girls outside laugh. They never sleep. The night is theirs.

I've lost possession of the night. All I possess is the darkness that seeps from the day, like the stench that seeps from a foul cheese. No one minds that I'm so impotent, no one pays me any mind, apart from Monika, my grisly benefactor, my darling, fumbling landlady. I rest and rest. But my strength isn't returned to me. My headaches steal me. I am to be left in peace as much as possible.

Monika gifts me a cat, it's white and called Pierre, I struggle to love it, but it doesn't seem to care, it snuggles up to my leg, flops down on my stomach to sleep and purr. It's a comfort.

I give off night scent. I'm a bit like an overripe apple. And I wonder if soon I'll fall from this tree that is life. Monika sends for the doctor. Her concern for my health swells. He examines me. He says I don't know what it is but it isn't dangerous, that he promises me, with his trustworthy smile and his nice, narrow eyes under those big bushy brows. I whisper, no. It's clear as day that he has no clue what to do with me, this eager disease, blackened ugly beautiful poor darling. This difficult patient. She who fades in the sunlight like clothes. He has no rational explanation to give. He tries with: You must have caught a draught, you must be stressed. Get some sleep. He prescribed a sedative.

My made-up face spills out onto the sheet; all my colours are there; red and black and beige. In sleep – a kind of peace at heart, even as wild animals with long, blue teeth stand before me smiling.

What do you think the animals mean? I ask Monika the morning after. She shakes her head and points up at the hideous red glass lamp that shines above us and makes the woodchip wallpaper blush, probably meaning God.

God knows. Eat up, my sweetheart, and I make it through an omelette.

Wobble to the toilet with dizziness around me like a feather boa. Reach out for something to hold on to, and land on a perfume bottle from the ornament shelf, drop it, and am falling, and it's crushed, explodes rose scent into the house. Then I throw up.

An old friend's, says Monika, who never smells of anything but bread and sweat, pay it no mind, she's long gone.

And I genuinely don't pay it any mind.

The girls below, they're healthy and sunburnt. They hum and lark. They're medicine too. If not elixir.

I can go to church with Monika, she allows that, and she lets me lean on her. My saintlike crutch hoping to make an impression on the priest. I am her halo. I shine light around her hair. Something new, something pretty. A relation? A niece? Henrietta? We walk arm in arm to her usual pew. The hymns are crazed birds flying across the sky to destinations unknown. I go a bit dormant as the mouths sing, there are many yellow teeth, many neglected smiles, and I look at the stained glass and the light that lights it up.

The bells ring, and the dog barks, the one in the garden, by the church, its black fur makes me want to be shiny and warm like golden jewellery in the sun. Sat a while on the bench in the park with Monika, looked at the apple blossom on the apple trees, and after some time, in which we exchanged no words but stared into space, or back at the apple blossom, a girl came whooshing past us on roller skates, headed for the ice cream stand by the lake, see that, she said, my Monika, licking her lips, as the knitting in her lap was red. The girl's dress was short and flew up, and her panties were black like the dog's, like Satan's eyes.

A child screamed and screamed and screamed. Blood ran from her knee.

Monika puts her hand on my thigh, come, let's go, and we go home, looking more like mother and daughter than I'd like us to, a father's shrill consolation in our wake.

My legs are weak, I wobble slightly, and a breeze cools me down. I'm walking with Monika, high-heeled, I still feel kidnapped by unease. In someone else's hands, a puppeteer's. My painted-on smile can slide off. It's as if, as if it will snow all of a sudden, even though it's summer, like the medicine the doctor gave me, like it's poison in my blood, not relief. Now I slowly peter out, now I'm naked, bathed in sweat, feverish, dying. Unless someone comes to my aid. Unless someone will rescue.

Take me seriously.

My trustability is not what it was when I was a child and was praised for those eyes that opened so wide and never lied.

My clothes are soiled. My appearance is unkempt.

Poor nerves, whispers the doctor in Monika's ear.

Monika, one moment quarrelling at me, the next purring for me.

I humour her as best I can, so I can lie under her wings and warm myself up like a duckling. It's the loveliest.

Monika's neighbour isn't home when we get back from the church. The phone rings and rings and rings. It rings all day, and no one answers the call.

A call that won't take not being answered for an answer is unsettling. I can't stand the sound of it, but I can't go out, I'm not allowed, not now, sweetheart, says Monika, she's sat with the paper, not reading it but gripping its sides like it's a rudder, she sails us away in the house, bound for shiny, beige trousers with wide legs and oven-fresh morning bread. You're too sick, sleep now, again, little one.

Or come and keep me company.

Her tights lie on the floor.

Her feet ache. She puts her naked foot in my hand like it's a present, tells me to rub hard so the blood can flow brisk through the body. I massage both feet thoroughly, she emits small moans of pleasure.

Says thank you, and that thank you means it's time to retreat to my room, to prevent any unfortunate little accidents.

Monika is easily annoyed, and I tend to provoke.

Forget to turn off the tap, so it overflows and the floor is wrecked, Monika mutters, and forget to lock the door and a thief can't believe his luck and walks straight in and out with Monika's precious antique gold watch in his rucksack.

She's so angry she doesn't speak to me for days.

But then I knock, at night, in my finest underwear, and show myself off a bit, as she lies and grumbles, and warms slowly up, and then we're ok again.

That's all it takes. Her spirits restored.

Down to the shop, together, for beers, for the girls, we amuse ourselves lining the cans up around the fountain, like a magic circle, and sitting down on a bench, both of us knitting, pretending not to notice the girls being lured in and drinking the beers in long swigs, unbeknown to their mothers and fathers.

They wobble around so drunk and shapely in the mild dark of the summer nights. They're not theatre, they're church. I clasp my hands and pray for them, that they may encounter bright futures with bright minds, like angels and larks.

My knuckles are ruby red.

Then there are hoodies to brood in.

Their eyes in them, like yellow animal eyes in caves,

like small light beams for the lost. So she can find the piece of bread in her bag.

I know they don't know I'm watching them. Or how.

I'm dirtier than Monika. But also purer, because what do I see other than myself. And I cry easily.

Who wouldn't want to fuck a 15-year-old girl, I once heard an ugly man say to a beautiful man in a dingy corner of the world, the lamps shone soft red, and there were rings from glasses on the wooden tables.

It moves me so when something is young and beautiful. Maybe pale too, a white forehead, feverish cheeks. A sick face. Mild and languishing.

The helpless who want to be helped and admired.

I get so excited and desirous. Consoled.

Want to bring everything to my breast, let every mouth suckle.

I have no children, I want to let everything be my daughters. Be everyone's daughter.

It's time I left Monika, and I don't know if I can.

She deifies me and her deification is a manger. Rocked softly to the end of its days.

I want to be too.

I can't say I'm not grateful. My life has borne me forth to images I can't take my eyes off.

My mirror image is a friend, she lays a hand on my forehead, and I draw consolation and courage from its warmth.

Now I'm young and old, ugly and beautiful.

When I look at myself in this mirror my smile doesn't cave. It shines a little.

That much I got. If nothing else. Fire, stars, muscles, breasts, sunsets. His eyes. And his.

Until now I'd believed the greatest threat to me was the eyes, because they can see me, judge me. But now I understand, I must understand, that no, no it's not the eyes, the ones that shine like headlights in forests, it's the hands, yes, the hands are the threat. The real one. They can take. They can flay. The eyes I can keep at bay with my chin up, head held high, pissing on the image I maybe am. But the hands are violence, if they want to be violence. And the hands that once reached out, just to touch, get a feel for, 'you're freezing', they didn't stroke, didn't only, now I see, they made the bruises bloom.
It lives under my skin, it's something to do with my blood, something wrong, it flows too slowly through my veins, increasing the risk of blood clots, making me dizzy at every turn, is this the work of the hands? Back then's hands? Who knows, says the doctor, the beautiful one, could be

anything, the body remembers, the body is more than it seems.

Yes, it's dream. I say. Bending slightly over, letting the heavy breasts fall.

The doctor leaves his phone number on a yellow note, says: You can always call, if there's anything, and the note is in the drawer in my bedside table and there isn't anything, I don't call, even though I want to feel his hand on my forehead again, two fingers on my wrist, counting. It's sexy. But I'm alone in feeling it, that this is red, soft, hungry. He's all seriousness. All work. No more women in fur collars and lipstick for him, it gets on his lab coat, can't be washed off, and his wife is depleted, like earth. Love is made.

In their house.

I have no business there.

No one gives me their heart, so I take what I can get.

Monika's hand.

Shelter.

Girls.

I'm safe in the sublime. In what can be dreamed up.

All that wears and tears at me can be pacified with glossy image power. Roses and angels. Glitter and snow.

A red-cheeked child, a bird.

Forthcoming

(type 2 – prose)
Mr Outside by Caleb Klaces (2025)
Happiness by Yuri Felsen, trans. Bryan Karetnyk (2026)
Hell of Solitude: Selected Writings of Ryūnosuke Akutagawa by Ryūnosuke Akutagawa, trans. Ryan Choi (2026)
Lamento by Madame Nielsen, trans. Gaye Kynoch (2026)

Back Catalogue

(type 1 – poetry)

Plainspeak by Astrid Alben (2019)
Safe Metamorphosis by Otis Mensah (2020)
Republic Of Dogs/Republic Of Birds by Stephen Watts (2016/2020)
Home by Emily Critchley (2021)
Away From Me by Caleb Klaces (2021)
Path Through Wood by Sam Buchan-Watts (2021)
Two Twin Pipes Sprout Water by Lila Matsumoto (2021)
Deltas by Leonie Rushforth (2022)
Island mountain glacier by Anne Vegter, trans. Astrid Alben (2022)
Little Dead Rabbit by Astrid Alben (2022)
Emblem by Lucy Mercer (2022)
Twenty-Four Hours by Stephen Watts (2022)
Journeys Across Breath: Poems 1975–2005 by Stephen Watts (2022)
Artifice by Lavinia Singer (2023)
Incubation: a space for monsters by Bhanu Kapil (2023)
Monochords by Yannis Ritsos, trans. Paul Merchant, with Chiara Ambrosio (2023)
Virgula by Sasja Janssen, trans. Michele Hutchison (2024)
The Grimoire of Grimalkin by Sascha Aurora Akhtar (2024)
rock flight by Hasib Hourani (2024)
Silk Work by Imogen Cassels (2025)

(type 2 – prose)

Fatherhood by Caleb Klaces (2019)
I'm Afraid That's All We've Got Time For by Jen Calleja (2020)
The Boiled in Between by Helen Marten (2020)
Along the River Run by Paul Buck (2020)
Lorem Ipsum by Oli Hazzard (2021)
The Weak Spot by Lucie Elven (2021)
Deceit by Yuri Felsen, trans. Bryan Karetnyk (2022)
Our Last Year by Alan Rossi (2022)
Vehicle: a verse novel by Jen Calleja (2023)
Lori & Joe by Amy Arnold (2023)
Pleasure Beach by Helen Palmer (2023)
The Earth is Falling by Carmen Pellegrino, trans. Shaun Whiteside (2024)

Prairie, Dresses, Art, Other by Danielle Dutton (2024)
The Seers by Sulaiman Addonia (2024)
Mountainish by Zsuzsanna Gahse, trans. Katy Derbyshire (2025)
Book of Mutter by Kate Zambreno (2025)
Appendix Project by Kate Zambreno (2025)
Fair: The Life-Art of Translation by Jen Calleja (2025)

(type 3 – interdisciplinary projects)
alphabet poem: for kids! by Emily Critchley, Michael Kindellan & Alison Honey Woods (2020)
The sea is spread and cleaved and furled by Ahren Warner (2020)
Songs for Ireland by Robert Herbert McClean (2020)
microbursts by Elizabeth Reeder & Amanda Thomson (2021)
Sorcerer by Ed Atkins & Steven Zultanski (2023)
I will pay to make it bigger by Ahren Warner (2024)
Diary of an Ending by Lina Scheynius, trans. Saskia Vogel (2025)

(type 4 – anthologies)
Try To Be Better ed. Sam Buchan-Watts & Lavinia Singer (2019)
PROTOTYPE 1 (2019)
PROTOTYPE 2 (2020)
Intertitles: An anthology at the intersection of writing & visual art, ed. Jess Chandler, Aimee Selby, Hana Noorali & Lynton Talbot (2021)
PROTOTYPE 3 (2021)
PROTOTYPE 4 (2022)
Strangers Within: Documentary as Encounter, ed. Therese Hennigsen & Juliette Joffé (2022)
PROTOTYPE 5 (2023)
Seven Rooms, ed. Dominic J. Jaeckle & Jess Chandler (2023)
PROTOTYPE 6 (2024)

(House Sparrow Press)

A Sparrow's Journey: John Berger reads Andrey Platonov (2016)

Infinite Gradation by Anne Michaels (2017)

Doorways: Women, Homelessness, Trauma and Resistance, ed. Bekki Perriman (2019)

Dialogue with a Somnambulist: Stories, Essays & a Portrait Gallery by Chloe Aridjis (2021)

Through the Billboard Promised Land Without Ever Stopping by Derek Jarman (2022)

A Finger in the Fishes Mouth by Derek Jarman (2024)

( ) (   ) p   prototype

poetry / prose / interdisciplinary projects / anthologies

Creating new possibilities in the publishing of fiction and poetry through a flexible, interdisciplinary approach and the production of unique and beautiful books.

Prototype is an independent publisher working across genres and disciplines, committed to discovering and sharing work that exists outside the mainstream.

Each publication is unique in its form and presentation, and the aesthetic of each object is considered critical to its production.

Prototype strives to increase audiences for experimental writing, as the home for writers and artists whose work requires a creative vision not offered by mainstream literary publishers.

In its current, evolving form, Prototype consists of 4 strands of publications:

(type 1 – poetry)
(type 2 – prose)
(type 3 – interdisciplinary projects)
(type 4 – anthologies) including an annual anthology of new work, *PROTOTYPE*.

Girlbeast by Cecilie Lind
Published by Prototype in 2025

(second printing)

First published as *Pigedyr* in 2022 by Gyldendal, Denmark

Published with the support of the Danish Arts Foundation

K:
Danish Arts Foundation

 A CIP record for this book is available from the British Library.

Based on design by Matthew Stuart & Andrew Walsh-Lister (Traven T. Croves)
Typeset in Marist by Seb McLauchlan
Printed in the UK by TJ Books

ISBN 978-1-913513-77-1

(type 2 – prose)
www.prototypepublishing.co.uk
@prototypepubs

prototype publishing
71 oriel road
london e9 5sg
uk